The Stone Of Gardar

Written and Illustrated

by

A. Wales

AWsome Books

First published in Great Britain in 2000 by
AWsome Books, 1 Wide Lane Close, Brockenhurst SO42 7TU

Copyright © 2000 A. Wales

ISBN 0 9539904 0 0

Printed in Great Britain by El Alamein Press Ltd, Salisbury

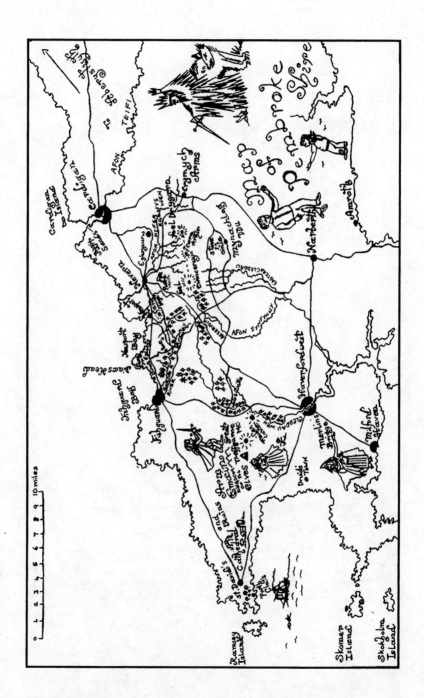

THE TRILOGY

The Stone, The Ring and The Shield

PART I
The Stone of Gardar

PART II
The Ring of Gyges

PART III
The Shield of Agamemnon

PART I

The Stone of Gardar

To Aurora –

With Best Wishes
from
Ann Wales.

Happy Reading
2003!

PREFACE

The Stone, The Ring and The Shield

It all began with a stone from St. David's, a large volume in Ancient Welsh from Aberystwyth University, and Peter and Sarah, who have been wanting me to tell their story for at least the last thirty years. My two shadow children had been with me ever since I began writing stories at school. They came into being properly during the family holidays in Wales.

Pembrokeshire, the Prescelly Mountains in particular, is a very strange place, with ancient monuments strewn around every few yards. One can well imagine that Elves or, in Welsh, *Ellyllon*, the Family of Beauty, are never far away. I always wanted to meet them and Peter and Sarah, through the power of the miraculous stone are able to do so.

The stories are rooted in a strong family background. We first meet the children with their Aunt Myfanwy (Aunt Myf) who usually has them for the summer holidays, while the children's archaeologist parents teach at University summer schools. Peter and Sarah are taken to visit St. David's and it is there that Peter discovers a strange looking stone, it is the *Stone of Gardar*. Little does he realise that it is a long lost treasure of the Elves of Arx Emain, a stone of great power and a portal to other dimensions. It is then that the adventures really begin!

The first book of this trilogy concerns the continuing battle for Power between Gwyn-ap-Nudd, King of Arx Emain and Lord of the Elves, and Arddu, the Dark One. The ancient Stone of Gardar could be an aid to either side. Its discovery by Peter is a vital element of the struggle.

When the war between the Elves and their adversaries is over, Peter and Sarah's Mother and Father, Dr. and Mrs. Jones, are brought to Wales. They meet Anir who is a long lost relation of Peter and Sarah's Mother and their Aunt Myf. He is the Guardian of the lands around Arx Emain (the magical realm of Gwyn-ap-Nudd). He accompanies Peter and Sarah on many of their adventures in his capacity as envoy between humankind and the world of magic.

During the course of the trilogy, the whole Jones family enlarges and evolves and strengthens its bonds. As archaeologists, Mother and Father Jones are frequently busy on 'digs' around the world, often in Classical Lands. Peter and Sarah often travel with them, enabling them to discover the ties between history, magic and mythology. Whenever ancient monsters are disturbed, they know they can rely on the Elves and their friends to help them out. As the miraculous Stone of Gardar makes time travel possible, the children meet many heroes from ancient times.

In book two, we are introduced to Merlin and King Arthur, inhabitants of Roman Britain! Peter and Sarah are called out of their own time to try and help King Arthur win a war against the Western Roman Empire, aided by the ring of concealment, *The Ring of Gyges*.

Book three opens as Sarah and Peter travel to Greece with mother and father. Dr. Jones is working on a 'dig' at Mycene. Peter and Sarah have fun at a beach resort with their cousins Emma and Amy.

Father Jones discovers the tomb of a warrior and much treasure including *The Shield of Agamemnon*. However, the 'dig' awakens Agamemnon, Cassandra and Demeter. Disasterously, Demeter follows the treasure back to Wales when the family returns home. It takes all the wit and power of Merlin, the Elves and their miraculous stone to defeat her.

I am afraid Merlin had to make a return appearance because Peter and Sarah think he is so nice and they have got to like him! He also insists on re-appearing in some of the other stories.

Whatever does happen in the following books, the Jones family will find it interesting, exciting and exhilarating, and I am sure that my young readers will again find it gripping, entertaining and enjoyable!

CHAPTER ONE

The Beginning of Everything

It was a hot summer in Pembrokeshire where Peter and Sarah were spending their summer holiday. As usual they were staying with Aunt Myf who lived in a cottage by the sea on the edge of a small village called Cwm-yr-Eglwys. So far they had spent a pleasant week exploring the sea shore, clambering over rocks to gaze in the still pools and venturing into caves, dark and exciting but not too deep.

"I should like to live here all the time," said Sarah, as she bounced about in the back of the car on the way back from Cardigan. Aunt Myf had taken them to the market. Peter agreed.

"And whatever should I do!" exclaimed Aunt Myf, "You are eating me out of house and home. Just look at this monstrous pile of shopping! Should last the week but I don't suppose it will with you two around."

They all laughed. Aunt Myf turned the car into the drive and it jumped and jolted all the way down to the cottage, where at last they tumbled out with the shopping. Aunt Myf prepared supper and when they had eaten Peter and Sarah made plans for the following day. They both felt they would like a change from the beach and the sea. Peter persuaded Sarah that they really ought to go and view the Prescelly Mountains.

"We could walk from end to end," he said, "starting before lunch and finishing before supper."

Sarah wanted to look at a map before she decided, and Peter showed her the track across the tops.

"It looks a very long way to me."

"We could start really early and take it easily," Peter was not to be put off. "It's the most mysterious and magical part of Pembrokeshire. We've simply GOT to see it!"

"Very well, then, but we shall need a picnic."

Sarah went into the kitchen, taking Peter's rucksack, which, with Aunt Myf's help she filled to the top.

"After all," she said, "we shall be out for lunch and tea."

Aunt Myf promised to drive them to the starting point and to collect them not far from the other side of the range, sometime near suppertime.

"Doesn't matter if you are late, I shall be waiting," said Aunt Myf. "And now you had better go straight to bed. Early to bed, early to rise, as they say. Goodnight to you both, sleep well!"

"Goodnight! We shall!" called Peter and Sarah, and off they went.

At eight o'clock Sarah awoke, slowly, until she heard the clatter of plates downstairs and saw that Peter's bed was empty. She was soon dressed and arrived in the breakfast room to find Peter buried in the Prescelly map with an empty plate beside him.

"Well indeed!" said Aunt Myf, "We thought you were never coming." Peter muttered something about an early start, but Sarah took no notice.

"Two eggs please," she called to Aunt Myf and sat down beside her brother.

Peter was still deep in the map when Sarah and Aunt Myf had washed up and put everything away. At last Sarah snatched the map away from him in sheer desperation. "Come on, you could have memorised it by now."

Peter sighed and got up.

"That is not such a bad idea," he grinned. "Fetch out the rucksack little sister and we'll be off."

Sarah made a face and groaned.

"O.K." she said, "I shall carry it half way and then you can take over. It will be a great deal lighter after lunch anyway; but knowing you it will soon be filled with interesting stones to go in your collection of fossils and axe heads."

Peter was interested in Archeology and thought he might like to follow in his Father's footsteps, but he was not always accurate in describing his finds. They were on the point of having a discussion, as Peter always described their arguments, when Aunt Myf swept them and the rucksack out of the house and into the car.

It was a fine, clear, sunny day. They drove through the little town of Newport, towards Nevern, then turned off on the road that leads to the Prescelly Mountains. At Tafarn Y Bwlch Aunt Myf stopped the car.

"The path is not far from here," said Peter, as they got out.

"Remember, I'll be waiting for you at Crymych about suppertime. Have a good day!" Aunt Myf said, as she handed Peter the rucksack and drove away.

Peter and Sarah walked along the road searching for the path. Before long they could see it, leading upwards from a lay-by. They crossed the road and began the ascent to Prescelly Mountain, the first peak in the Prescelly range of hills. It is a long way, and before long Sarah was wanting a rest.

"Let's stay here by this stream, we could dip our feet and have something out of the picnic."

"We are not even half way up," said Peter.

"You said it wasn't far."

"Well it isn't! There by lunchtime, I promise!"

Peter strode onwards and Sarah had regretfully to leave the stream and follow him. They rounded the edge of a forest and came in sight of the concrete pillar, which marks the highest point.

"It's after midday," said Sarah.

"We can have lunch on the summit. Once we're up there we go straight across the peaks until we come to a hill fort and then it's down to Crymych."

Peter took Sarah by the hand and half pulled her up towards the pillar. A few minutes later they stood gazing at the view.

"Worth the climb?" questioned Peter.

"Marvelous!" Sarah answered. I do believe I can see St. David's."

They stood silent for a while, looking out over nearly all South Wales. Eventually attention was turned towards the rucksack and lunch.

The sun was hot and high overhead when they finished eating. Sarah said she would rather sit where she was for the rest of the day, as Peter spread the map out to show her where they were going next.

"What strange names," said Sarah, as Peter pointed out the names, "Even Prescelly Top has another one: Foel Cwm Cerwyn, I suppose 'Foel' is another name for mountain?"

"Yes, and 'Carn' obviously means Cairn. Now we must get a move on. It's afternoon already and we have hardly started."

Peter got up. Sarah packed what was left of the picnic, which was not very much, into the rucksack and off they went. As they came off Prescelly Top, they looked down into the Old Quarry where it was said The Blue Stones for Stonehenge had been mined. Mists curled far below them, giving an air of impending menace to the whole area.

Sarah shivered. Little did either of them know just how much of a part that Old Quarry, and indeed the Prescelly Mountains, would have to play in both their lives from now on.

The next mountain in the range was lower than Prescelly Top, so they had to go down before climbing up again. This was a nuisance and Sarah could see that the other peaks were similar and that they would be going up and down for miles.

"How far is it right across?" she asked, panting rather.

"Oh, about seven or eight miles, I should think."

Peter reached the top.

"This is Foel Feddau!" he shouted down at Sarah.

"At last!" What a strange place this is," Sarah yelled.

The path wound down away between stones scattered over the tops, as if some giant had sown them there, indeed the whole place was like some weird Moonscape. It was the oddest place she had ever encountered.

"Yes," said Peter, " it's more like something from outer space.

He ran down and in among the stones. On either side the mountains fell away into broad valleys. The land to their left looked flat and brown.

"Marshland?" queried Sarah.

"Yes, probably."

They spoke little now, as they had begun to climb again. Even Peter for all his enthusiasm began to wonder how long it would take to reach Foel Drygarn, the hill fort at the end of the Prescellys. They went on past Carn Bica and Bedd Arthur. Peter explained that Bedd Arthur meant Arthur's grave.

"He's got a Cairn as well," said Sarah.

They had stopped to look at the map.

"Yes he has, but we can't look at everything today."

All round lay huge piles of stones looking half natural, half as though someone had put them there. Many mysteries surround the Prescelly Mountains, as Peter and Sarah knew well.

Their Father, who was interested in old legends, had often told Peter and Sarah about them. One of the most enduring is how the famous Prescelly Blue Stones were transported to Stonehenge. By whom and how it was done nobody quite seemed to know!

"The road we are following now is Roman," Peter said, in way of explanation.

"Does it go to the Hill Fort?" Sarah asked.

"No, silly! Foel Drygarn is much older, prehistoric ---- Hey! Mind out!"

Peter had begun to lecture Sarah in order to explain about the ancient peoples who had inhabited Wales and the dwellings they had built, and especially Hill Forts. But all of a sudden, Sarah caught her heel in a tussock of grass and went flying into a patch of damp bog. She landed with a squelch.

Peter ran up to her, anxiously.

"Are you hurt?"

"No, I don't think so, only muddy. The bog round here doesn't seem to dry up, even in summer."

Sarah brushed the mud off where she could and they plodded on. They passed many more piles of wierdly stacked stones before at last they came to Foel Drygarn. A place filled with atmosphere and the reek of a history that had on occasion been an extremely violent one.

"Are we climbing again, Peter?"

"Yes, but this is the last one."

And up the slope they went.

"I think," said Sarah, as they stood on the top, "that Wales must have invented the ancient monument. Not two steps can we go before we fall over some cairn, or standing stone, or barrow, or ---"

"Or hill fort!" completed Peter. "It must have been quite a size, judging by what's left. You can still see where the hut settlement was here."

"So you can! But don't let's stay here too long. My legs are telling me that when they sit down it will be for good, and my stomach is telling me that it could do with some supper, and another thing ---"

"What?"

"This place gives me the creeps! It's really, really spooky! And I don't think I like any of the places up on these hills at all, especially round by that Prescelly Top!"

"Sarah, that's complete rubbish," said Peter.

But he had to admit to himself that there certainly was a strange atmosphere about the place, so they half ran down the hill, as if a thousand Ancient Britons were after them, not stopping until they were through the gate which opens onto the road to Crymych.

They looked back. Even in the bright evening sunshine Foel Drygarn managed to look dark and oppressive.

It was in fact well past suppertime when they stood wearily at the door of Aunt Myf's car, which she had parked outside the Crymych Arms. They got in. Aunt Myf asked Peter if they had enjoyed themselves and they both began to tell her about the walk.

After a while Sarah fell fast asleep in the back of the car. They were hardly through Newport. She did not wake up until they were back at the cottage and Peter had to shake her hard to get her to move!

The next day it rained. Peter and Sarah were glad in a way because it gave them an excuse to be lazy and do nothing all day. They decided they needed a rest after the previous day's long walk.

Peter was full of ideas about what they could do next and Sarah was content just to sit and listen to him.

"How about St. David's?" he said, as they settled down to watch the rain dripping down the windowpanes in the drawing room. They had just had a very large lunch.

"How about it?" said Sarah.

"It would be very interesting to see the Cathedral. Let's ask Aunt Myf to take us there."

"What! This afternoon! I thought we were having a lazy day."

"It would be nice to go this afternoon, but I meant tomorrow, actually," said Peter, lamely.

"Well, I suppose it wouldn't be much fun in the rain, but go and ask Aunt Myf anyway. If we stay here all day we might get tired of doing nothing and die of boredom."

Sarah sat down in one of the large armchairs and waited while Peter went to ask Aunt Myf if she felt like going out. They were surprised when she said that they might as well go that afternoon.

"The wireless said that the rain should clear by early evening and we could have a look at the ruins of the Bishop's palace," Aunt Myf said, as she looked for her umbrella.

Peter and Sarah struggled into mackintoshes, and went out to the car. It was still raining when they arrived at St. David's.

"Present structure begun in 1180."

Peter was reading the guidebook in a loud whisper as they stood in the nave. He continued to give Sarah the guided tour, until by the time they came out of the Cathedral, the sun was shining through the clouds and Sarah thought she had heard quite enough about St. David's. Aunt Myf seemed to think so too, and returned to the car.

"But we haven't seen the ruins at the Bishop's palace yet!" said Peter.

"That's quite all right," said Aunt Myf, "I shall wait for you here. My poor old feet have had all they can take for now. You two go off and enjoy yourselves."

So Peter and Sarah ran towards the ruins. They spent a good hour climbing up and down walls and old staircases, of which there appeared to be several.

"I declare this to be the best ruin we have ever seen!" said Sarah, "Because it has so many stairs and a ruin is much more interesting if one can climb to the top of it."

Laughing, she ran up one of the longest flights of stairs to look out over the palace. The clouds were drifting away, seawards, westwards. Far below her Peter was engaged upon enlarging his collection of ancient stones.

He had collected a few chips from a heap of rubble where some of the walls were being restored. Then he saw IT! A stone shaped like a pyramid, with an opening cut into the upper third and with strange marks upon the base. It was sky blue in colour and was not too large to hold with one hand.

"Wow! This looks precious!" Peter muttered under his breath, "I wonder how the builders can have missed it. It must have belonged to someone in the palace long ago and have been hidden away. Yes, somewhere where no one could ever find it, inside this wall! What a good thing they knocked it down. What a find! I've never had anything as good as this before."

He looked round to see if anyone was watching and then quickly put it in his pocket. Just in time, for with the sun came more tourists and the builders who were restoring the ruins came out of a hut to return to their work.

"Aren't you coming?" he called to Sarah.

Somehow he felt that the stone was something very much out of the ordinary, more than just a valuable addition to his collection. He decided to show the stone only to Sarah for the present.

"Come on little sister!" he called, "Hurry up!"

Sarah jumped down the last two steps.

"Oh Peter! You are irritating sometimes. You know I don't like you calling me 'little sister'."

She frowned at him meaningfully.

"I've found something rather special."

"What is it? Oh! I think I can guess! It's some of your silly old stones. Well, don't blame me on the way home if they weigh a ton, I'm not carrying any."

"They are all small, just bits and pieces really, but one is absolutely extraordinary! I'll show it to you later," he whispered, as they reached the car.

That evening, after supper, Peter and Sarah went up to their rooms early. Peter had his stone collection arranged on the windowsill, but the St. David's Stone he had hidden away in a box in the suitcase under his bed. It was the only stone that he kept from the Palace, for he had thrown the others, stone chippings from the wall, away in the garden. He brought his prize out triumphantly. When she saw it Sarah was most impressed.

"Goodness! Whatever do you suppose it is?" she said, as Peter handed it to her.

"I don't know. I have never seen stone like this before, but I think it might be lapis lazuli and that means it must have been part of the Palace treasure or a jewel belonging to one of the Bishops."

"Have you noticed the strange marks on the base of it? They look like scratches but they are in groups and must have been made on purpose."

"Yes, I know what you mean, I think they are letters. They could be prehistoric writing, even Ogham perhaps. I am sure I have read about it somewhere."

"Yes, so have I. It's in the guide book downstairs. 'Ogham: the writing that was used by the ancient British and Irish.'"

They stood silently looking at the stone for quite a while, then Peter put it back in its box and into the suitcase under the bed.

"I feel somehow that we ought to keep this stone a secret. Don't tell Aunt Myf or anyone else about it."

Sarah stared at him, amazed. The first thing Peter did usually when he thought that one of his stones was a great discovery was to tell the whole family about it, and anyone else who appeared interested.

"Why ever not?" she gasped.

"Just a feeling," he said, as he shrugged his shoulders, "as soon as I saw it, I knew it was something mysterious."

"Could we not try to solve the puzzle of the writing? That would be one mystery out of the way," said Sarah, who by now was feeling rather curious.

"Very difficult! Even if we found out what the letters were, we probably wouldn't understand what they said."

Peter sighed and yawned.

"Let's think about it tomorrow," he said, and they prepared themselves for bed.

When Sarah awoke next morning, Peter was sitting by her bed, the Stone in his hands. He was staring fixedly at it.

"Still puzzling?" she watched as he got up to go and put it away again.

"It's fine again today, Peter, let's go up to Carn Ingli common, it looks a bit less foreboding than Foel Drygarn."

"Right!" Peter replied from deep within the suitcase, "I expect Aunt Myf will run us there, if we ask her nicely.

They delayed the visit until after lunch as Aunt Myf said that she wanted to go shopping in Newport in the afternoon, as the town was as a rule a little less crowded in the afternoon than in the morning.

"On a day like this," she said, "everyone will be going to the beach."

When they arrived at the bridge on the road below Carn Ingli, it appeared that they were not to have the common to themselves. There were several cars.

As they jumped the bank and crossed over a small stream, they could see some people with a dog walking towards them. There was also a party of hikers striding over the Carn Ingli hill fort.

"I rather hoped that we should have the common to ourselves," said Peter.

"Never mind!" said Sarah, comfortingly, "By the time we reach Carn Ingli they will be well on the way back. I expect we shall miss them."

It was quite a steep climb to the first cairns and Peter and Sarah rested awhile on the highest to get their breath back. Then they climbed over the slabs of rock and stood and looked out over Newport bay. There was a pleasant breeze and after crossing the Prescelly Mountains this walk was more like a stroll than serious walking. Beneath the hill fort itself Sarah found bilberry bushes. It was too early to look for berries but she managed to find one or two, juicy and sweet.

They went then to Carn Ingli hill fort. Sarah was wrong on one point, although it was not as large and did not look as foreboding as Foel Drygarn, it too had an atmosphere about it.

"There is the hut settlement below us," said Peter, as they climbed over a wall at the top.

He pointed to ring upon ring of stones, spreading away down towards the road to Newport. Sarah was looking over to Foel Drygarn.

"Not far as the crow flies," she said, "I can see Prescelly top too."

"Yes Sarah, I noticed as we came there is a fine view of Prescelly Top from between two groups of rock, almost like a window."

As he was speaking, he caught a glimpse behind one of the ancient ramparts of a man very strangely dressed. He wore a grey cloak over a tunic of deep crimson. Pinned on one shoulder was a silver brooch. He was leaning forward, as if to try and catch what Peter was saying. Sarah saw him and cried out.

"Hey, you! What do you want?"

"I'm sure he's been listening to us," said Peter.

They were both looking straight at him when he disappeared.

"Come on Sarah, he must have ducked down when you shouted at him. Let us go and rout him out."

"Why do you think he was listening to us? And why did he look so peculiar?"

"I'm sure I have no idea why," said Peter; "but looking or listening he is not here now. There is no one behind the wall. He must have gone to hide in one of the hollows. I'm going down."

Peter ran back towards the common and Sarah kept close beside him, as she felt rather afraid. She was very glad when they arrived at the base of the hill fort and after scanning it for some time, could see nothing.

"He must have gone down the other side. It looks rather too steep to explore properly," said Sarah.

"We couldn't catch him now anyway," Peter said, feeling rather breathless by this time.

"Perhaps he wasn't looking at us at all."

"Well, I am quite certain that he was. If he wasn't, why should he run away?"

"I don't know," Sarah said, crossly, "and I don't think I want to know. Talking of running away, let's go back. I've had enough of this place, strange listeners and all!"

Sarah started to walk away quickly. Peter glanced back at the hill fort but he could see nothing there except the stones; so he followed her. They both felt relieved when they got to the bridge and were safely on the way to Newport.

CHAPTER TWO

Ederyn

Later that evening, during supper, both Peter and Sarah were
unusually silent. They were thinking of the strange man who had
been listening to them on Carn Ingli hill fort. Peter could not
help feeling that somehow the strange stone that he had found at
St. David's had something to do with it.

Aunt Myf noticed that they were uneasy and tried to cheer them up. She suggested they play 'Snap' after supper and Peter and Sarah agreed, glad to do anything that would stop them pondering over the peculiar events of that afternoon.

Before they went to sleep, Peter took out the stone from it's hiding place under his bed. He could not stop turning it over and over in his hand, looking at and examining every part of it.

"I wish I could put it somewhere where I know no one else could ever find it," he thought, "I would carry it in my pocket but it might fall out, and I would hate to lose it. However, it's no good, I'm too tired to think about it now."

He slipped the stone under one side of his pillow and fell asleep. He was restless and one of his dreams was particularly vivid. In the morning he could remember it clearly and went straight into Sarah's room to tell her about it.

"We were both in a hall of stone, surrounded by wonderfully carved pillars of stone. There was gold everywhere, but the strangest thing of all was the niche behind what I think must have been a great golden throne."

"Oh! Quick, tell me, tell me!" cried Sarah, and jumped out of bed in excitement.

"Inside the niche was my Stone," Peter grinned triumphantly.

"Is that all! Well I'm beginning to wish you had never found it. If you are not talking about it, you are thinking or dreaming about it. Let's think about what to do today. I would like to go seal watching. You know the little bay, not far from here, Aunt Myf was saying last night that if we wait long enough we could watch them play."

"OK, then, we'll do that."

Peter could see that Sarah was quite adamant and gave in gracefully.

"No more talk of the Stone?" she said.

"Absolutely none! Come on, let's go to breakfast. I smell bacon."

After breakfast they packed up the rucksack again. It was soon filled with sandwiches and cola cans and the binoculars, for a really good view of the seals.

They said their farewells to Aunt Myf and set off along the cliff path. The morning breeze died away and Peter was glad when they came to a tunnel of trees and tangled undergrowth, giving shade as the sun climbed. Sarah loved the walk. Every now and then she stopped to pick the wild summer flowers, or to peep through the branches of gorse and bracken for a glimpse of the sea.

"There are a lot of boats out today. Most of them look like fishing boats. Couldn't we go fishing one day, Peter, it would be such fun."

"Mmm! I suppose it might be."

Peter did not sound very enthusiastic. Neither of them could sail a dingy and the thought of rowing in the hot sun was not his idea of time well spent.

"We would have to borrow nearly everything, including any fishing tackle. Really, Sarah, it wouldn't be worth it. Besides, Aunt Myf promised to take us to Skomer or Skokholm Islands. We shall get the boat from Marloes harbour and the trip to the Islands is quite long. Much more fun than fishing and you get to see the Puffins. Just wait and see. Aunt Myf says that we might go next week."

They walked on in silence for a while as the track led them down to the bay where the seals were. They crossed the beach and climbed up a very narrow, steep track to where a stile led into a hay field.

"It will be quite all right for us to go in. At least the hay is cut and we shan't do any damage," said Sarah, as she jumped down from the stile.

"No need to worry, Sarah, Aunt Myf knows the farmer here. She has permission to cross here any time and she trusts us and knows we wouldn't do any damage."

In any event, they kept the country code and walked well into the side of the field. Then their way led downwards and out of the field and to the rocky cliff below. Peter and Sarah went carefully down, until round a corner they came to a large slab of rock, rather like a table top, jutting out into the sea. Upon one side it fell sheer into the sea.

An inlet, rather like a small fjord had been carved by the waves. Its furthest cliff was alive with nesting seabirds. This was where the seals came to play. Upon the other side of the rock slab there was a way down to the sea, but Peter decided it was too difficult for them to attempt, certainly before lunch, at least, and so they stayed where they were.

It was midday and very hot. After they had eaten all of what was in Peter's rucksack, they stretched themselves out on the rock slab and waited for seals to appear. They were not to be disappointed that afternoon.

Sarah was the first to see one, then another came and the pair played and swam round the rocky table for most of the afternoon, most enchantingly. They came quite close to where Peter and Sarah were lying. Sarah watched the seals eagerly until they decided to leave, and swim out to sea again. When she turned round at last, she found that Peter had disappeared.

"He's got fed up, I suppose," she thought, "bother him!"

In fact, the last time she had looked round, Peter had been fast asleep. However, a short while later, he woke up and decided to get up and stretch his legs, leaving the rucksack and binoculars behind for Sarah to carry, if she wanted to follow him.

Sarah put the binoculars in the rucksack, which she slung over one shoulder and began to climb back up to the hayfield. She was feeling rather angry with Peter for having left her alone and not telling her where he was going.

"One good thing," she muttered under her breath, "he can't have gone far, because it must only be about half an hour at the very most since I looked at him and had it in mind to prod him awake."

Peter had decided, once he was fully awake, to play a trick on his sister. He had got up very quietly. Sarah he could see was engrossed with the seals. He felt too hot for comfort and thought it might be cooler in the shade of the bushes, which were on either side of the stile.

Sarah would notice his absence eventually, and she would have to come over the stile on her way back. Then he would leap out of his hiding place in the bushes and surprise her.

Peter strode up the edge of the hay field. He was deep in thought, visualizing the look on Sarah's face when he caught her unawares. He did not see the person who sat looking intently at him from his perch on top of the stile.

Peter came to the stile and looked up; into a pair of piercing blue eyes. He stopped short with a sudden intake of breath. The person before him was like no one he had ever seen. Besides the blue eyes, which he felt were looking right through him, the face looked friendly: young, but seeming to reveal a great wisdom. It was surrounded with fair hair, gleaming in the sunlight.

The Elf, for Elf he was, smiled and then spoke softly, his finger upon his lips.

"We meet at last. Come with me."

He motioned to Peter to climb the stile and then crept into the bushes. Peter followed him, too amazed to say or do anything else. They sat down among the roots face to face.

"I saw you on Carn Ingli Top. Who are you and what do you want?" questioned Peter.

"That is the whole point of the matter, something that is of very great interest to me and my kinsfolk."

"What is?"

"That in these modern days you and your sister can see me at all! However, you have an honest look about you, so I shall take the risk and hope nothing ill may come of it. My name is Ederyn and I am brother to Gwyn-ap-Nudd, King of the Elves in this southernmost realm and Lord of Arx Emain that was once called Golden Hill by some of your ancestors. Now, tell me who you are."

Peter gasped and rubbed his eyes. He thought, perhaps, that he was still asleep and dreaming but the Elf Lord sat before him, showing no signs of disappearing. Ederyn raised one eyebrow indicating that he was waiting for an answer.

"My name is Peter," said Peter nervously, "and my sister is called Sarah."

"Is she following you?"

"Er, well; yes she is, I think, in a little while."

Peter blushed and stammered with embarrassment. He did not like to tell the Elf Lord of the rather feeble trick that he had been going to play on her.

"Well, we shall wait for her here and then she will be doubly surprised!" Ederyn grinned.

Peter had a suspicion he knew all about the trick. He blushed a second time, almost to the colour of Ederyn's tunic.

"It is a great mystery to me how..." said Ederyn, then broke off what he was going to say, "Listen, here is your sister now, if I am not mistaken."

He got up swiftly and in one movement almost, swung out his arm from the bush, plucked Sarah from the stile, rucksack and all and sat her down beside her brother. She did not just look surprised; she looked terrified. Peter turned towards her.

"Hi, Sarah, this is Ederyn and he is an Elf Lord."

"And you are Sarah," said Ederyn, "and now that we have all been introduced, we had better get down to business. As you saw, I was on guard at our watch post on Carn Ingli. Anything strange or unusual I must report. Well, nothing stranger or more unusual than your good selves being able to see me without my willing it has happened for years uncountable! I am afraid that, having made my report, the Lord Gwyn-ap-Nudd requests your presence before him at Arx Emain. He will then decide what is to be done. Seen by humans, indeed!"

Ederyn got up.

"Will you come with me?" he asked.

"Is it far? " said Sarah, looking very anxious still, "And how shall we go?"

"From here to Arx Emain is just a little under ten miles, as the buzzard flies. Do not worry, we are going to ride. My horse is waiting for me in the forest, close to that farm. He shall bear us all easily. Sarah shall sit before me and Peter shall sit behind. We will walk to the forest along the line of this hedge and thus avoid being seen. Now, what do you say, Peter? Will you come?"

There was a slight hint of urgency in Ederyn's voice.

"We will go with you," Peter said.

Sarah shot Peter a look of total disbelief, but Peter suddenly felt excited. Something within him very much wanted to visit the Lord Gwyn and Arx Emain.

He looked at Sarah, she was still looking very anxious, but she nodded her head at him. In fact, Sarah was growing more curious by the minute. She had several questions to ask Ederyn but for the present there was not time to do so.

Ederyn pulled his grey cloak about him, hiding the crimson tunic completely. He led them out of the thicket where they had been sitting and then, as he had suggested, along the side of the hedge, which ran along the rim of the hill. They passed from the hayfield through to one filled with corn.

Sarah noticed that Ederyn made no noise when he walked and hardly bent so much as a blade of grass. As they followed him, Peter and Sarah tried to do the same, with little success. They would need a great deal of practice to walk as softly as the Elves.

Once within the forest, Ederyn soon found his horse. It was a fine looking beast, grey, with a dark mane and tail.

"His name is Tad," said Ederyn, and leapt up onto Tad's back.

"Give me your hand, Sarah."

He pulled her up and seated her before him.

"Come Peter," he said, and Peter was soon seated behind him.

Peter noticed that there were no stirrups on Tad for Elven horses do not require them, they are so tamed by their riders. Only in times of war will the Elves use them as an aid to defeating their enemies, but they have never really needed them.

"Hold fast to my belt, Peter, and we shall be off!"

So saying, Ederyn whispered his instructions to Tad, who sprang away at a brisk trot through the forest. They followed a stream, then crossed the main Newport road. Fortunately, there was no traffic in sight. Then up hill and down dale they went, for miles and miles.

Tad galloped where he could over broad commons and along ancient tracks. They crossed the Gwaun Valley and forded the river. Peter guessed that they must be going almost due south west, down towards Haverfordwest.

Sarah plucked up courage and asked her questions.

"Why is Carn Ingli so important?"

"That, Sarah will need a long answer, but since we have at least an hour's ride still before us, I may be able to tell you a part of it. Gwyn may tell you more when we reach Arx Emain. In the past, in the long distant past when Carn Ingli and Foel Drygarn were mighty fortresses; we Elves still had business with the men who lived in this realm. Over the years, more and more since those times, men have gone their own way. They have become suspicious of us and we could not trust all of them either! So now, in these modern times, they mind their own business and we mind ours! We do not meet with menfolk at all unless we wish it. No man may see us or visit us without our permission. However, you saw me when I did NOT wish to be seen, so perhaps things are changing. We have a common enemy to deal with. The Dark One, Arddu! We shall need all the help we can get to bring about his utter defeat. Menfolk should be ready to help us again as in my view they were partly to blame for his arrival in these parts. We have always been reluctant to meddle in the affairs of men, but occasionally it is necessary if they need saving from themselves. Then, also, if they need to be saved from something that they have started and which has got quite beyond them. How often have they dipped their fingers into things that did not concern them. Then, when disaster looms, they leave others to clear up the mess!"

Ederyn looked down at Sarah.

"I'm sorry," he said, "I should not be giving you a lecture. I was thinking aloud and that is most unusual for an Elf. Thought travels swifter than words, as we say."

Peter managed to hear most of the conversation and remembered how Ederyn had known about his 'surprise' for Sarah, without having been told of it, From now on he would have to be very careful what he thought about.

"Why are you taking us to Lord Gwyn?" asked Sarah.

"Because," said Ederyn, "whereas all the visitors to Carn Ingli that afternoon saw nothing, you did! The Lord Gwyn would very much like to meet two children who have such sharp eyes. As soon as I told him, he became interested in you and sent me back to seek you out."

"Is there much further to go now?" Sarah then asked him.

"Just a step."

Tad had slowed to walk and then halted at the meeting of several roads.

"In a moment we shall be riding along the banks of the western Cleddau, then we shall pass into the forest that you can see from here. Within the forest lie the Halls we made long ago. No stranger has been within them for many an age, only those who are very specially privileged. Now you will see them! They are magnificent! On, Tad!"

It was not many minutes more before they came to the hill, in which lies the main entrance to Arx Emain. From the outside it did not look at all impressive.

"Just a hill with a few old holly trees around it," thought Sarah.

Ederyn dismounted and then helped Peter and Sarah down from Tad's back. He walked towards the trees. The children followed with Tad behind them.

"Here we are," said Ederyn, pointing to the side of the hill where two large and extremely gnarled holly trees grew, side by side.

Between the two trees the grass grew greener, as if it were tended like a garden lawn. Behind the trees rocks formed pillars and a lintel. As they came closer, Peter and Sarah could see that doors had been opened and were now lying flat against the hillside. From within the hill came a tall Elf, armed with both sword and spear.

"Who comes to Arx Emain? " he said.

"Hail Eldol, it is I, Ederyn. I have brought the two guests to see Lord Gwyn."

"My Lord Gwyn is waiting in the outer hall. He is anxious for news and his temper becomes shorter by the minute!" the tall Elf frowned.

"We shall go to him immediately," said Ederyn, beckoning to Peter and Sarah to follow.

Eldol stood aside to let them pass and as they crossed the threshold, another Elf came from the shadowy passage to take care of Tad.

Inside there was dim light. There were torches, and occasionally lamps on the walls, but they were few and far between, but even so, Peter could see that the passage they were walking in was very wide and had many tunnels leading out of it. As they came to the end he could see more light coming from a great archway of carved stone.

Ederyn led them under the arch and into what Peter guessed rightly was the outer hall. There were many Elves in the hall seated on benches round the walls. As Ederyn entered with Peter and Sarah they rose in greeting. At the other end of the hall was a dais with four carved wooden pillars from floor to ceiling, in the centre of which was a carved wooden chair.

In the chair sat Gwyn-ap-Nudd, Lord of Arx Emain. He looked very much like his brother, Ederyn. Neither Peter nor Sarah could imagine how old either of them were.

The Lord Gwyn was dressed in clothes that seemed to change their hue as one looked at them, or whenever the Elf Lord moved. He wore a massive golden belt from which hung a sword, its sheath covered with many jewels, and round his neck he wore a chain of gold with a single blue stone upon his chest. He got up from the chair and came down from the dais.

"Welcome my brother!" he said to Ederyn, "you have done well, I hope?"

"My Lord, here are Peter and Sarah."

Ederyn brought them forward.

"I am sure they will tell you all you wish to know."

Gwyn returned to his chair upon the dais. Two stools were brought for the children and they sat on either side of him. Ederyn sat upon the step of the dais, listening.

"First," said Gwyn, "my apologies for having had you brought here in such haste, but you may come to understand later that I had good reason to do so."

Sarah cast a glance round the hall. None of the other Elves present seemed to be looking at them or taking any notice of them. Indeed, after their arrival, most of them had left the hall. There were only a few remaining, and they seemed to be either asleep, or deep in thought. She looked back at Gwyn.

"Did you know of us, or were you looking for us?" he asked Peter.

"No," said Peter, "we were not looking for you, in fact all of this has been one surprise after another."

"It all seemed to start when Peter found that strange looking stone at St. David's," said Sarah, suddenly.

"What stone? What did it look like?" Gwyn looked suddenly stern.

"Well," said Peter, who after the encounter with Ederyn had rather forgotten about his 'find', "it is blue and looks like a pyramid, with a hole in the top of it."

"Ah! And were there any markings on it?"

"Yes," said Peter, "on the base of it. I think it's Ogham, but we had not got as far as trying to find out what they mean."

"Well done, Well done indeed! You have found it at last" cried Gwyn, leaping from the chair.

"Did you hear that, Ederyn? I am sure these children have found the Stone of Gardar that we have sought down all the centuries. It is a good thing you did not translate the Ogham. Had you done so, you would have brought down all the power of the Samildanach upon you and that is something that not even I would do in a hurry. The words on the stone are only to be spoken aloud in times of direst need. Do you have it with you, I am anxious to see it again."

"Oh no," cried Peter in distress! "I left it behind. I am afraid it is still at Aunt Myf's."

"Then I hope most sincerely, that you have it in a place of very great safety."

Peter's face fell as he remembered what he had done with the stone. Instead of hiding the stone away as usual, he had left it under his pillow.

"Well, Er not exactly," he said.

Gwyn turned to Ederyn.

"Then all is not well," the Elf Lord said, looking anxious, "but we must not be in so much of a hurry to regain what we lost so many years ago that we forget caution. In St. David's you found it? That is very interesting. However, Ederyn and I must take council at once to decide what is to be done; apart, that is, from sending you back to collect the Stone as soon as possible. The Stone will not be safe until we have it here. While Ederyn and I discuss this matter, you Peter and Sarah shall rest here and be refreshed. Come Ederyn!"

So Peter and Sarah were left sitting on their stools in Gwyn's outer hall, and wondering what was going to happen next.

A few minutes after Gwyn, Ederyn and the Elves who had been waiting in the hall had left, a tall man entered. He was followed by an Elf woman who carried a tray of food and a jug of clear water.

"Welcome!" the man said, " It is not often we have guests here. My name is Anir and this is the fair lady Aneryn, who brings you bread and fruit. Something to take the edge off your hunger until you return home. I have been sent to entertain you while you eat, and then I shall escort you back to the house of your Aunt. The lord Gwyn tells me you have found a mighty treasure that we had thought lost for ever; he said also that you might like to know some of its history."

"We should like that very much," said Sarah. "but..." she paused.

"You may eat."

The lady Aneryn proffered the tray of food and exchanged a look with Anir.

"Is it safe?" Sarah asked.

She had read a fairy story once, where children had been enticed into the fairy castle by the food out of which it was made. Once they had nibbled at its outer crust they were hooked, and having consumed their fill of the goodies, they were never able to leave Fairyland again. Was this normal food, she wondered?

"It has never done me any harm," laughed Anir.

Then he seated himself on the step of the dais to begin his tale. Sarah observed that he was gaunt and lean looking. His dark hair fell almost to his shoulders and was rather unkempt. In fact he looked as though he had been without a change of clothes for a very long time.

He was dressed all in brown, and one could hardly tell in places where mud ended and cloth began. His eyebrows were black and bushy and met over his nose. Under them, his eyes were blue and almost as piercing, Sarah thought, as those of the Elves.

The Lady Aneryn stood behind the two children and smiled to herself as Anir began his tale. She was really beautiful. The children were both quite astonished at her beauty. Her long chestnut brown hair fell down below her waist. She was wearing a simple sky blue dress with a silver girdle. Her gaze seldom wandered far from Anir.

"I think," Anir began, "as you came here Ederyn mentioned to you the name of our enemy; Arddu, the Dark One. Now he has caused trouble in these lands for so long that only the Elves remember how it all started, or even how he came to be here at all."

Anir sighed. Peter was wondering how a man (and such a strange man at that!) came to be with the Elves. Anir continued:

"When men first came to the Prescelly Mountains, many, many ages ago, they were mighty warriors from eastern lands. They had traveled far, conquering nation after nation as they went. Elves were here before them and waited for some years before showing themselves. As is usual with their folk, they were able to pass unnoticed among the menfolk until they wished to be seen. Very proud were those warriors. Their chief delight lay in weapons, treasure, and the carving of stone. Many of the ruins of their work are still to be seen. I am sure you have noticed quite a few. They are sill very impressive."

"You mean the strange stones we keep finding? However did they manage to lift those huge ones that we see in the stone circles and burial mounds?" asked Sarah, fascinated.

"The Dark One was anxious to gain power over the warriors from the moment that they arrived. You see, they had tremendous wealth and they wanted to show all the world how great and powerful they were. Before Arddu came they built great stone monuments indeed. Then Arddu promised to help them. After the men accepted his services the monuments grew larger and greater still. For a while they had been friendly with the Elves because of the Elves' great power and because the Elves gave them gifts of the like they had never seen before. However, in the end the Dark One took them over completely and ruled them. The Elves hid themselves again and waited. Years passed and the Elves heard that Arddu had gone with all his warriors to a great war, away south and west of here. It was somewhere between Stonehenge and Avebury. Arddu and his warriors were defeated and most of his great army were killed or injured. He fled back to the Prescelly Mountains for refuge. There he had made himself a secret fortress underground and there he stayed for years uncountable. The Elves still feared that he might be dangerous and kept watch over the Prescellys. When the men of Stonehenge came to remove his fortress gates, taking them for war booty, the Elves came to help them. Unfortunately, instead of driving Arddu out of the mountains, they only drove him further in. So they decided to block him up inside the mountain. They left him there, imprisoned for ever, or so they thought."

"What exactly happened to the fortress gates?" asked Peter, although he thought he could guess.

"Why!" exclaimed Anir, "The men of Stonehenge took them away and made them part of their mighty temple, to remind Arddu that they had overcome him. But, he was not so easily vanquished. The Elves have always been aware of his desire to make mischief among men. My Lord Gwyn journeyed north to his kindred in the land of the Summer Stars. He went to the Islands of the Samildanach, the many skilled and to him they gave The Stone of Gardar. That is the stone you have just found! The Samildanach gave it to Gwyn to be a help to him, should he have any further dealings with Arddu. Not only that, but it strengthens the power Gwyn has already within his kingdom. You must understand that it is for Gwyn to use it against Arddu, but it has other uses too though I do not know what they are presently. It has been lost for too long and even the Elves may have forgotten. However, know that if Arddu ever finds it, he would not be able to destroy the Elves. They would become weakened, so that eventually they would have to flee from their halls. Then no man, woman or child would ever be safe here again."

"But if the stone was so valuable to the Elves, how on earth did they manage to lose it?" said Peter.

"Well," said Anir, "it was many long years before men settled in these parts again. They were farmers first, but proud warriors also with bright swords and spears. It was they who built the hill forts. Carn Ingli and Foel Drygarn are only two of them! They began to have trouble with Arddu straight away, for he had not been idle in his prison under the mountains. He had collected an army of underground creatures over the years and made many entrances and exits to his dark land. The chiefest of these we call Deorath, or the dark gate. Again, men asked the Elves to help when they found out that Arddu was planning to attack them. Elves and men then watched and waited in the hill forts. All seemed quiet, for a time. The attack came suddenly to Carn Ingli and to Foel Drygarn at the same time. Gwyn-ap-Nudd's brothers Ederyn and Elidir had each gone to defend one of the forts. Both the forts were very hard pressed. Arddu and his creatures would certainly have won that time if Gwyn had not taken the Stone to Ederyn at Carn Ingli where they were able to defeat the enemy at last, with the help of the Samildanach. Then they left for Foel Drygarn, but were too late to save Elidir and the men who had held the fort with him. I do not believe the full power of the Stone was used at that time, I also think that the Lord Gwyn regretted that. Arddu retired once more to his Dark Kingdom, defeated for a second time but not destroyed. Gwyn built a cairn for Elidir and they mourn him still. On that day in the ruins of Carn Ingli, the Chief of the men who had survived the battle swore an oath to Gwyn. He swore that should Arddu come forth from Deorath again, or should any of his creatures be seen outside the Evil Kingdom, then he; or his descendants would fight for Gwyn. He also promised that men would help the Elves to guard Arddu. The chieftain's name was Auvandil and his oath has not been broken, even in these days."

Anir paused and looked up at Aneryn.

"Yet the Stone was lost," she said.

"Yes," said Anir, "during the battle for Carn Ingli Gwyn kept the Stone, but when he, Ederyn and Auvandil rode to Foel Drygarn Ederyn had it. In the confusion they met when they arrived at the Fort, somehow it fell somewhere and was lost. A watch was set upon Prescelly Mountain and Deorath, and all of Arddu's Dark Kingdom. In time most men forgot the battles and now they hardly remember the Elves. Although here they are often referred to as the 'Family of Beauty' or the 'Ellyllon'. They keep to their farms and leave the old places alone."

"Who watches the Dark gate now?" asked Peter.

"The Elves keep constant watch, and I am of some use also, I hope," said Anir, getting up.

The children had finished eating and the Lady Aneryn took their mugs and plates and left the hall.

Gwyn and Ederyn returned and Anir went to greet them. Peter turned to Sarah:

"Who would have thought that my stone would turn out to be so important!" he said.

"I wish we had brought it with us," said Sarah. "I keep thinking of that awful Arddu. I can just see him grabbing it from under your pillow. Why did you have to leave it there?"

She had no time to say more, for Gwyn, Ederyn and Anir were coming towards them. They had evidently come to some decision. Gwyn spoke:

"Peter and Sarah; you will ride now with Anir to the house of your Aunt and collect the Stone. I should like you to return tonight, naturally, but we might upset your Aunt if you did so."

"We shall be rather late back now as it is." Said Sarah, "I think she will be a little upset already."

"Be that as it may," replied Gwyn, "You will be quite safe tonight and you can return here, as soon as you are able, tomorrow morning. Anir will see to it. Ederyn will return to Carn Ingli and more of my people will be sent there and to Foel Drygarn. Arddu will be suspicious if he or his spies have seen you with Ederyn. He will be even more so if you are seen with Anir. I impress upon you, Anir, the seriousness of this matter. Please be extra careful, especially after what you and the scouts saw last night."

"Farewell to you, and a safe return!" said Ederyn.

"Farewell; until tomorrow," said Gwyn.

Anir then led Peter and Sarah out of the outer hall and down the long passage to the front door where an Elf waited with a horse for the return journey.

After they had mounted and the horse had begun to pick its way through the trees, leading them away from Arx Emain and the city of the Elves, Anir spoke. Although he smiled at Sarah, she could see that he was worried.

"A rather garbled account of the Stone's history I gave to you, back there in the hall. I am sorry there was not time for the full story. If you ever return to Arx Emain for a longer stay, Gwyn or Ederyn would tell you more."

As before, Peter sat behind and Sarah sat in front. Peter clung to Anir as his horse, urged on, galloped over some open moorland.

"What is the time?" said Sarah, half to herself, as the slowed to cross a stream.

"It is eight o'clock by the sun," replied Anir, "I gather you fear an angry relative!"

"Oh, Aunt Myf? Well, we did say that we would be back in time for supper and that should have been at least an hour ago."

"Well, we shall soon cross over Carn Ingli Common and I shall be setting you down at your Aunt's door. I shall not return to Arx Emain tonight, for Gwyn has given me the task of guarding you and the Stone."

Anir was as good as his word and they were back in Dinas not long after.

When Peter and Sarah arrived at Aunt Myf's house, Peter decided to tell her that they had gone to sleep on the rocks where they had been watching the seals. They found Aunt Myf in the kitchen with a salad supper waiting on the table. At first she looked cross, then she looked relieved.

"Well!" she exclaimed, "You didn't tell me that you wanted a late supper! I had begun to be a little anxious. I have already eaten mine. You two tuck in. Whatever happened to make you so late?"

"We just fell asleep on the rocks," said Peter simply, "it was very hot."

Aunt Myf asked no more questions. Peter felt relieved. After all, it was partly true. He had gone to sleep on the rocks, even though Sarah had not.

After supper, Aunt Myf sent them straight to bed. Peter was soon asleep. Through her door, Sarah could hear him muttering in his sleep as he turned over:

"Elves and Stones and Golden Hills and..."

The muttering trailed off into silence. Sarah was glad that, when they dashed upstairs after supper to look for the Stone, it was still where Peter had left it, under his pillow.

The next morning, the children woke excited. It was the first of August. The fine weather looked set to continue for some time. But, most important of all, they were to return to Gwyn and the Elves with the Stone. That is, as soon as they could possibly do so.

Peter left the Stone under his pillow again when they were dressed. He had been looking at it again with renewed interest while Sarah got ready. Then they went down for breakfast, which they decided would be a quick one. Afterwards, they were to go straight away to meet Anir, whom they knew would not be far from the house.

"He means business all right!" said Peter, "Did you see? Under his cloak he wore a long sword!"

Peter looked up at Aunt Myf, but she was gazing absentmindedly into her teacup.

"Well and so!" she said at last, "I have to go into Haverfordwest this morning. Do you want to come? It's business for me, I'm afraid, but you could walk round the shops. Then we could go round the old castle ruins in the afternoon. How about it?"

She looked at the two children. Peter looked at Sarah. They had to refuse; Anir would be waiting.

"No thanks, Aunty," said Peter, " I think it's going to be too hot for shopping today and we got awfully hot yesterday. We will be quite all right here."

"Are you sure? What about you Sarah? I thought you might want an outing somewhere."

"No, really. We're not very fond of Haverfordwest anyway. It's not as pretty as Cardigan or Newport."

Sarah hoped their excuses would put Aunty off. Aunt Myf nodded.

"I suppose you are right, although I do like the shops there very much. I must be off now. I'm sure you don't mind if I leave you with the washing-up, just this once."

She got up from the table and went straight to her room to get her bag and gloves. As soon as they heard her door shut, Sarah looked at Peter and groaned.

"What shall we do? We have all this to clear and wash up, the Elves to go and visit with your wretched Stone, and then we have to be back here before Aunt Myf. If we keep disappearing all the time she is going to get suspicious and I'm sure she won't swallow tales about Elves, Golden Hills and..."

"And miraculous Stones!" said Peter. "No, I see what you mean. I wonder where Anir is?"

He jumped round as Aunt Myf came in through the kitchen door.

"Bye, dears. See you later on, after lunch sometime."

Peter and Sarah watched as she walked briskly out into the garden. After a few moments they heard the car start and then go off down the drive.

"Tell you what, Peter, you go and look for Anir and I'll make a start on these breakfast things."

Peter needed no second telling. He ran out into the garden. He had no idea where Anir might be, where Anir spent the night, or how Anir was to contact them that morning. Peter saw something move in the small copse at the end of the garden hedge.

Something told him to stop running. He was not more than a few feet away from the hedge and the branches of the beech trees that grew in the hedge spread their fingers over him. Behind the hedge came the noise of breaking twigs and rustling leaves. Someone or something was coming towards Peter.

CHAPTER THREE

The Breath of Orddu

Peter stood stock still. Although the weather was hot, Peter felt a cold chill creeping over him. He wanted to run away but remained where he was, as if commanded to do so. The feeling of dread and terror in the pit of his stomach made him nearly physically sick.

A long dark shadow crept from the bushes, like a hand reaching out for him. Peter's head swam and the whole world began to revolve.

"Hey! Hey! What goes on here?"

Anir's voice rang out -- like the beam from a lighthouse in sea mist, Anir broke through the darkness that now surrounded Peter and the far end of the garden. Anir leapt behind the bushes and laid about him with his dagger. The darkness disappeared and Peter fell to the ground in a faint. Sarah ran across the lawn.

"Peter, Peter!" she cried, then knelt beside him and shook him by the shoulders in an effort to rouse him. "Wake up Peter, what's wrong? Oh do wake up!"

Anir returned from the copse looking pale.

"Is he all right?" he asked.

"Oh Anir, what happened? What is wrong with my brother?"

"I am not sure," replied Anir, "but it is likely to be some evil spell of the witch Orddu. I have given her something to think about just now with my dagger and my sword, Carnwennan. It once belonged to King Arthur and there is some magic for good in it still."

Sarah began to cry.

"I bet this is something to do with that stupid stone of Peter's, or the Elves, or whoever it belongs to!"

"A good guess!" said Anir. "Where is the stone now?"

"Under his pillow."

"Go and fetch it then, now, hurry!"

Sarah sped away as if the witch were after her and soon returned with a cloth bag in which was --

"The Stone!" whispered Anir.

Peter stirred but his eyes remained closed.

"What do we do now?" asked Sarah.

"I will try something," Anir replied, taking the stone from Sarah.

After a silence of several minutes, he held the magic stone a few inches above Peter's forehead and began to mutter strange words. As he did so, after a while, Anir began to sway rhythmically from side to side. Sarah looked at Peter. Nothing seemed to be happening.

Anir began to sing softly under his breath and as Sarah watched there came a faint glow of light from around the hole at the top of the stone. Suddenly, Peter gave a very deep sigh and smiled in his sleep. Anir put the stone back inside the cloth bag and placed it in his tunic pocket.

"I think your brother may improve shortly," he said, with not a little relief in his voice.

"But he is still asleep!" said Sarah.

"Yes," said Anir, "but I have removed the evil of Orddu out of it. To awaken him we shall have to take him to Gwyn. Let you and I carry him back to the house and then we can take counsel in hiding, while we may. We cannot remain here too long, else Orddu and her creatures will be back for us."

Anir put his strong arms under Peter's shoulders and Sarah picked up his feet. Together they walked down the garden path and into the kitchen. Sarah motioned with her head for Anir to come into the sitting room, where they placed Peter gently on the sofa cushions.

Anir drew all the curtains and began to pace up and down the room. He looked strange and out of place in Aunt Myf's pristine, modern sitting room with his mud spattered clothes and battered boots.

"We must go to Gwyn at once," Anir said, half to himself, "but how?"

"Couldn't we wait until dark?" said Sarah, "then nobody would see us."

"Oh, but Orddu and her kind certainly would. Their power is greatest in the dead of night."

"I see," said Sarah, wanly.

She was just going to ask if Anir had any idea what they were going to do, when a noise distracted her. It was the sound of a car drawing into the drive, Aunt Myf's car.

"Oh no!" cried Sarah, "it's our Aunt. What will she say about Peter?"

She looked at Anir and half expected him to gallop out of the house and hide among the bushes in the garden. Anir showed no sign of leaving. Sarah looked around helplessly. Surely Anir did not belong in Aunt Myf's world, nor she in his.

Sarah heard the click of the front door as it opened and Aunt Myf came in, laden with shopping. She grunted as she put down the heavy bags. Sarah ran out to greet her.

"There you are, Sarah. Help me with these bags, there's a good girl. I forgot to take my Building Society book with me. I'll have to go another day. What a nuisance! I'm so forgetful these days. I don't know why, I think it's because I have too many things to think of at once, especially with you and Peter here. Now where is that boy? He can just come here and give us a hand."

Aunt Myf paused as she and Sarah got the bags set down on the kitchen table. Sarah was desperately wondering how to explain what had happened to Peter when Anir peered round the kitchen door and then came in. Aunt Myf did not look at all surprised. It was Sarah who was surprised when all Aunt Myf said was:

"Oh, it's you. What's up?"

Anir shook Aunt Myf by the hand and sat on the kitchen chair. "It's your nephew, Peter. I have reason to believe that Orddu has put a black spell on him because of something he found. An ancient treasure which belongs to the Samildanach."

"Oh really," said Aunt Myf, putting on the kettle, "and what is that then?"

"The Stone of Gardar," Anir said, drawing the stone from its bag in his pocket. Peter is sleeping now, but we must take him to Gwyn-ap-Nudd as quickly as we can."

The stone glowed faintly in Anir's hands. He placed it swiftly back in the bag and replaced both into the tunic pocket again.

"And where is Peter?" asked Aunt Myf.

"Oh Aunt Myf, he's on the sofa. He won't wake up at all. What are we going to do?" wailed Sarah.

Aunt Myf strode into the sitting room and went to kneel beside Peter, who was still smiling in his sleep but showed no sign of waking up.

"Oh what a nuisance you are."

Aunt Myf stroked his cheek gently.

"Well, well! Anir, Anir, come here."

Anir came and stood in the doorway.

"Anir, look -- if you must take him to Gwyn-ap-Nudd for a cure, I can drive you and Peter as near to Arx Emain as I can. Maybe the Haverfordwest side would be safest."

"Aye, Lady, that would be wise but what shall you and the girl do? Orddu has been drawn here by the Stone or sent here by Arddu. It makes no difference, she knows that the Stone has been here and may return to seek for it again."

Sarah stared at the two of them. It was dawning on her that Aunt Myf must be one of those very rare grown-ups who can inhabit two worlds at once and is at ease in both the 'real' world and the 'other' world. At any rate, she appeared to know Anir quite well, and showed no signs of panic or astonishment at the present turn of events.

The kettle began to whistle and Aunt Myf sprang into the kitchen. She made a pot of tea and directed Anir to the hall cupboard to fetch the heavy travelling rug in which to wrap Peter.

"In case he's suffering from shock," she explained.

When Anir reappeared, he asked her again:

"What will you do, Myfanwy?"

Aunt Myf put the tea things and a plate of Belgian buns on a tray and marched into the sitting room again. They ate and drank, sitting in a semicircle round Peter.

"There's only one answer to that!" said Aunt Myf, "My family is the most precious thing to me in the whole world. I don't have one of my own, yet, but I may some day. Meanwhile, my sister's children have brought joy into my life and I would not desert Peter for a second. So, if he goes to Arx Emain, so do I and so does Sarah."

"But Gwyn-ap-Nudd has never met you!"

"Yes, but you know me, Anir. I have played among the stones up on the Old Places since you and I were both children. And if the Family of Beauty don't like it, they will have to lump it! If they want their Stone back they will have to put up with the consequences. After all, if you can pass in and out of Arx Emain, then so can I."

"Yes, Myfanwy, but for me it was decreed. It has been the duty and the joy of all my forebears to be The Guardian. You were not chosen."

But Aunt Myf was not to be moved.

"I go!" she said, then, "How are you, lovely?" to Sarah.

"Oh, I'm all right, I suppose. Can we go now? I DO want Peter to wake up."

"Very well, little maid," said Anir, patting her shoulder.

Aunt Myf gave her a hug. Then all was action! Sarah and Aunt Myf put the shopping away: having asked Anir if food was required for the journey. He said 'no' as the Elves would feed them, if necessary, at Arx Emain.

Peter, wrapped in the travel rug, was carried out to the car and laid across the back seats. Sarah was to sit in the front seat with Aunt Myf and Anir said that he would curl up on the floor behind the front seats. Even with a cushion or two he did not look at all comfortable, but said he was used to rough circumstances.

When the passengers were all settled, Aunt Myf locked the house and got into the car herself. It was now getting on towards midday. The car started; she drove as fast as she dared towards Fishguard and from there towards Haverfordwest.

"I'm going the long way round," she said, "I don't fancy going near the Old Places today, so we'll give the Gwaun Valley a miss."

Sarah stared at the road ahead. She was petrified. Would they be tracked? She clenched her fists over the strap of Aunt Myf's handbag, which she had on her knee. Her knuckles were white and so was her face.

Anir did not move the whole of the journey. Eventually, Aunt Myf found a large lay by that she considered safe for her car. She and Sarah got out. Then, with Anir's help, managed to get Peter out. The car was locked. Anir hid behind the car with Peter in his arms, while Aunt Myf and Sarah watched the traffic pass, looking for a gap when they could cross the main road in safety. Of course it was very busy as it was a main road and the traffic was heavier than usual with many summer tourists. After what seemed like an age to Sarah, Aunt Myf gave a sign to Anir and they half ran across the road and dived into some bushes.

"I lead from here," said Anir, and strode away into the undergrowth, which was very unpleasant with brambles and nettles and large gorse bushes.

"Ow! Ow!" cried Sarah, "Not so fast. I'm getting prickled to death."

"Better than being prickled with a knife from one of Orddu's creatures," said Anir, curtly.

He held Peter in a kind of Fireman's lift and was obviously very strong as carrying her brother did not appear to Sarah to impede his progress one wit. On the other hand, Aunt Myf was having her difficulties. She had on a pair of sandals, which were even worse at letting in prickles and nettles than the plimsolls that Sarah was wearing. Soon she was lagging behind.

"Come on, Myfanwy," urged Anir, "through that copse and up to that hill to the left of the woods. We shall soon reach Arx Emain and then we can all have a rest."

"Come on Aunt Myf!" called Sarah, and she ran back to take her Aunt Myf by the hand and pull her along.

They were all very hot. It was just after midday; the sun was overhead and even Anir began to pant a little as they climbed towards Arx Emain.

Sarah looked back towards where they had left the car. The bright sunshine gleamed on the chrome bumper. She looked up to the cliff under which the car lay. A mist seemed to lie on the bushes at the edge of the overhang.

"Look!" she cried. There's fog on that hill. Anir turned his head sharply. "What in the world---!"

"It's creeping down to the car!" exclaimed Aunt Myf.

For a moment they all stood transfixed with horror, as the mist slid down the cliff face and into the lay by.

"Come on!" Anir called them back out of their stupor.

Sarah began a sprint that took her to the edge of the trees that formed the copses and spinnies around Arx Emain. Anir and Aunt Myf followed close behind. Anir was grunting because he was beginning to feel the weight of carrying Peter. A bramble made Sarah pull up.

"Ow! It's got my leg."

"Come here; let me see," panted Aunt Myf, who was beginning to wish that she had walked more and used the car less in recent times.

Sarah was extracted, painfully, from the bramble. Anir placed Peter down on the forest floor while Aunt Myf operated. Anir looked about. The forest was very peaceful and sunlight filtered through the trees, casting dappled shadows on Peter's still sleeping body.

"I'm sure he looks greener," said Aunt Myf, "or is it the light off the trees?"

"This is a good place for a bad happening," said Anir, who stood listening to the forest sounds. All at once---

"Down both of you!" he dropped to the ground.

Aunt Myf and Sarah followed suit.

"What...?" began Aunt Myf, but Anir shot her a look that made her stop asking any more questions.

Soon they could all hear 'swish, swish'. Footsteps, something approaching through the undergrowth and suddenly there was---

"Tad!" cried Sarah, as Ederyn's horse stumbled through some thick brambles towards them.

"Ederyn!" cried Anir, "And just in time too. We are being followed."

Ederyn jumped down from his horse. He needed no instructions for straightaway he picked Peter up, set him upon Tad, mounted behind and spurred the horse into as fast a trot as it could manage under the circumstances.

"Come," said Anir, "Peter is safe now and we shall be shortly."

"Why," asked Sarah, "Arx Emain must be miles away yet."

"So it is," Anir replied, "but I think we shall have assistance in getting there safely. See, here is Eldol to meet us."

"Ho there, Anir! You come sooner than expected."

And out came Eldol from behind a large beech tree.

"But not soon enough brother."

"Trouble again? I'll take the little maid. Here come hup! Eldol will let you ride pig-a-back for a while."

Sarah did as she was told. Aunt Myf took Anir's arm and off they went through the forest as fast as they could to Arx Emain.

The afternoon was wearing on as they stumbled out of the final clearing and could see Arx Emain and the holly trees that marked out where it was. As they approached, Eldol, who had been carrying Sarah again, placed her gently on the ground and hurried forward to the gate.

Before long, Sarah saw the gate open a crack under Eldol's hand. Then it swung fully open. Sarah hurried forward. Aunt Myf and Anir ran to catch up and came in close on her heels. Eldol waited for them all to pass into Arx Emain and then shut the gate behind them. Sarah breathed a sigh of relief.

"I could do with a nice cup of tea right now!" said Aunt Myf.

"I don't think these people drink tea..."

Sarah's voice trailed off into silence as Anir passed by with Peter in his arms. What could Gwyn do? Would there be a cure for the dark sleep that he was in?

She followed him with Aunt Myf behind, her footsteps slapping coldly on the stone floor. Every now and again a torch or lamp lit up the stone walls of the palace that was inside Arx Emain.

Strange inscriptions and marvelous designs were upon every wall and ran down the ceilings also. Sarah wondered at them as she passed, but was presently too preoccupied with her thoughts of Peter to take it all in.

Anir went down a passage to the left, to a room where there were several beds. He placed Peter on one of them. Immediately an Elf maiden appeared with a silver bowl filled with water.

"I am Morvith," she said, "Gwyn sent for me that I may care for your brother."

"I can care for Peter very well myself!" Aunt Myf said forcefully.

The Elf maid looked surprised.

"But!" she said.

"I'll take that bowl."

Aunt Myf made a grab for the silver dish, took it to where Peter was lying and began dabbing at his forehead with the cloth that was soaking in the water. Morvith disappeared into the corridor.

"I wonder if she's upset?" thought Sarah.

After about a quarter of an hour, Anir returned to them. Sarah was sitting on the floor beside Peter's bed. Aunt Myf sat on the bed. She had put the bowl of water on the floor and was now holding Peter's hand, deep in thought.

"Come, come! This will not do at all," said Anir, "food and drink await you. Gwyn-ap-Nudd will come soon and we will do our best to awake Peter from this spell."

Morvith appeared at the door again.

"Morvith will wait here with Peter. He is quite safe now. Have no fear for him and do come and eat."

Wearily, Sarah and Aunt Myf obeyed. Anir led them to what Sarah supposed must be the main hall of the palace. High arches, which glittered with thousands of precious stones, formed a huge dome.

Underneath was a dais with a throne for Gwyn; there were also tables where lay the evidence of a recently eaten meal. The odd silver dish and cup were being cleared away. This was indeed The Great Hall of Arx Emain.

During her sojourn with the Elves, Sarah noticed that the metal most favoured by the Elves for every-day items was silver, but for special things and places there was always a liberal and impressive spreading of gold.

To one side of the Hall, there was a table fresh laid, with food and drink ready. Anir and Aunt Myf sat down straight away. Sarah paused, she thought she did not feel very hungry.

"Come on Sarah," said Aunt Myf, "the soup is delicious and the bread is better than I make myself."

As her Aunt tucked in with gusto, Sarah sat down and joined the feast. She discovered that after fright and flight she actually felt very hungry indeed. Whether it was lunch or tea or

'TEANCHEON' Sarah was not quite sure but the meal filled every expectation.

There was vegetable soup with crusty bread and butter; followed by meat pasties with gravy and potatoes. There were fruits and some kind of heavy fruit bread, or was it cake? It was rather like the Bara Brith that Aunt Myf made for a tea time treat. The whole was washed down with water or a light fruity wine. Sarah, it must be admitted, had some of each!

When they had eaten their fill, some of the Elves came to clear away. Anir got up and said that Aunt Myf and Sarah had better rest while they could, he had business with Gwyn.

Sarah and Aunt Myf he led to a room close to where Peter lay. There were settles filled with cushions and heavy wooden beds filled with feather mattresses and quilts. Nightlights glowed in small niches carved into the walls. Sarah watched Aunt Myf kick her shoes off and collapse onto one of the beds.

"Get some sleep child," she whispered, and was soon snoring.

Sarah soon followed suit.

It was many hours later that Sarah awoke. They had arrived in the late afternoon. For the first time Sarah looked at her watch; it was half past eleven. She still felt very tired and for a while lay back in the feathers, half-asleep.

A little while later, it must have been around midnight, she heard a commotion in the next room. Aunt Myf was missing from her bed. Sarah jumped out of bed, slipped on her shoes and went towards the noise. It was Peter!

The Lord Gwyn was bending over him, muttering strange words, a light was in his hand. Aunt Myf was holding Peter's hands and looking worried. Anir stood in the shadows by the door and the Lady Aneryn had come and was holding the Miraculous Stone above Peter's head. It glowed with a strange and eerie light.

Sarah stopped dead in her tracks as a fierce beam of light sprang from the opening in the stone. Just for a second, it seemed as if the aperture widened to form a kind of portal, a gateway behind Peter and the bed. The sight was truly astonishing!

Peter screamed; the archway and the light disappeared. Gwyn-ap-Nudd sat down on a stool by the bed. The whole scene became calm. Sarah came into the room. Peter's eyes were flickering.

"He will wake soon, now," said Gwyn, who then rose and bowed to Aunt Myf then left them.

Anir and Aneryn followed him.

"He is waking up," Aunt Myf smiled as Peter's eyes opened.

He stared at his Aunt, then at Sarah.

"Where on earth?" he seemed to be taking in his new surroundings.

"You are quite safe now, dear," said Aunt Myf, "you had a nasty shock."

"Oh, no! The witch! I remember. She was muttering something horrible. I must have blacked out."

"So you did," Sarah said, patting his hand, "and caused us a deal of trouble, but you look better now you are awake."

"How long was I blacked out?" Peter frowned; he was puzzled.

"Oh; only most of yesterday," said Sarah.

"You'll have to tell me later. My head feels fuzzy somehow. I think I could eat something, though."

"That's our Peter," laughed Aunt Myf. "I'll go and see if there is anything."

She kissed Peter on the forehead and disappeared down the corridor. Peter sat up and held his head.

"What a headache! This must be what a hangover feels like."

"Well," said Sarah, "it's all to do with that odd stone. You would pick it up wouldn't you! It belongs to the Elves, you know. The Enemy wants it and that witch is a friend of his."

"Don't remind me," said Peter, and sank back on the pillows. Aunt Myf reappeared with a bowl of hot broth and some bread.

"This is all I could find this hour of the night," she said.

Peter sat up again and Sarah plumped his pillows. He ate the bread and soup greedily. It was, if they had known it, nearly dawn.

"I'm still tired," said Sarah. "I'm going back to sleep. Take care, brother mine, See you later."

She kissed his hand and went back to bed. It did not take her long to return to sleep, but before she did, she found herself thinking of what a great nuisance this adventure had been.

"If we're not careful, this holiday will be completely taken up with the wretched thing. I want to get back to the beach. Elves and stones..."

Her thoughts then passed into dreams. The next thing Sarah knew was someone shaking her by the arm.

"Wake up, wake up Sarah."

It was Peter.

"Peter," she cried, and jumped out of bed and hugged him.

"Steady on, Sis. It's nearly lunchtime. You had better not miss it. You've already missed breakfast."

"Why? Whatever is the time?"

"I just told you," said Peter, "nearly time for lunch; and I tell you, I'm starving."

"Again? Oh well," Sarah sighed, "I suppose you have to make up for all the meals you missed yesterday."

"I know, Aunt Myf has filled me in with everything that happened. But: I have some news for you."

Sarah began to dress.

"Well, what is your news? Aren't you going to tell?"

"Well," said Peter, slowly, "I think I'd rather show you."

And a few minutes later, they were going down one of the many stone corridors in the Halls of Gwyn-ap-Nudd. At length Peter turned sharp right, down a tunnel that Sarah had not yet discovered.

At the end of it the passageway opened out to reveal two huge doors that were very richly carved. Peter gave them a gentle push and they gave way before him, softly and silently. Sarah gasped. The huge room was quite empty and was lit only by two lamps hanging from the ceiling.

"It's just like the dream you had, isn't it," she whispered.

And so it was. Down the room forming an arch were two rows of stone pillars, richly carved with all kinds of trees and plants. At the furthest end was a niche behind a most splendid chair, which they assumed must be one of the thrones of Gwyn-ap-Nudd.

Everywhere there was the glint of gold, Welsh gold. In particular, the throne itself was very ornate, as was the niche, which glowed with a pale green light, the source of which appeared to be---

"Our stone!" Sarah said softly.

Peter looked at Sarah.

"This makes me feel, somehow, as if we were meant to come here."

He climbed the stairs of the dais, upon which the golden throne of Gwyn rested. Then, going up to the niche, he stared at the magic stone. Sarah followed. The stone looked quite normal, except for the greenish glow coming from it.

Both children stared at the stone for quite a little while, then turned and went to sit on the steps of the dais, where they gazed around at the wonders of the golden room. At last Peter touched Sarah's arm gently and broke her reverie.

"Come on," he said, "lunch."

And silently they tiptoed out of the room and shut the great doors behind them.

CHAPTER FOUR

Choices!

Aunt Myf was already in the dining hall eating her lunch when Peter and Sarah arrived. She was sitting with Anir, who was wearing his cloak ready for travel, and Aneryn, who was looking very solemn. Aunt Myf smiled at them.

"Come on you two, we have started without you."

"Where are the others? Where is Gwyn?" asked Peter.

"They will come soon," answered Anir.

"Come," said the Lady Aneryn, "there is roast lamb, vegetables, salad, a pork pie, bread, cakes and much fruit. Please, eat well."

For a while they gave all their attention to the food. Aunt Myf was chewing on an apple when Anir leant across the table.

"There is much we have to discuss," he said. "we will go to your rooms..."

A rustle of feet interrupted him. Gwyn and his Elves came into the Hall. Anir bowed as Gwyn passed them. Gwyn paused.

"We must speak with you later, Anir," he said, and made his way to the high table.

Anir ushered Aunt Myf and the children out. Aneryn followed behind. Down the passageways they went, back to where they had slept the night before. Peter and Sarah made for Peter's room but Anir pulled them out and pointed to the room where Aunt Myf and Sarah had slept, as it was larger.

They jumped on Aunt Myf's bed and got comfortable. Anir sat on a stool. Aunt Myf settled herself on the bed between Sarah and Peter.

"And so!" she said, questioning Anir with her eyes, "Can we go now or can't we?"

"That is a very difficult question, lady," said Anir, "I have been scouting with Ederyn this morning. I am afraid THEY have attacked your car."

"What!" cried Aunt Myf.

"It is quite burnt out," Anir said, matter of factly.

Peter and Sarah looked at each other anxiously, expecting Aunt Myf to faint or throw some kind of tantrum. Aunt Myf did nothing of the sort. She was horrified, but managed to retain her composure.

"At least none of us were inside it!" she said, "I shall have to claim on the insurance."

"Also," said Anir, "there are reports that your house may have broken into. Orddu's work, of course."

"Then it is a good thing we left it when we did," Aunt Myf said, keeping a very straight face.

Peter and Sarah had never seen her like this before and they began to see their Aunt in a new light.

"The question is," Anir looked round at each of them "what to do now? Gwyn is preparing to cross the sea to his kindred, in order to seek their aid. Ederyn will ride north, to the Elves of the High Places. A great army will gather. It is to be my place to guard Arx Emain with Eldol, for the present at least. It will take time to bring all the armies together. I will not be able to watch you all the time if you are 'out there'. Although, Elves could be posted near to you as protection."

Anir said this thoughtfully, as if he were trying to form a plan.

"But I will not be able to be with you unless you are in very great danger. Hopefully, Orddu will have reported your disappearance to her master. Arddu will naturally assume that you are here. He knows he cannot make a direct assault on Arx Emain, not unless the Elves were very much weakened. That means you are safe as long as you remain here. It is my counsel to you, that you stay here until Gwyn returns from gathering his armies."

"But I can't," wailed aunt Myf, "the local Police must have noticed the car and someone may have reported the break-in at my home. I at least must go and clear everything up."

"That could be arranged," said Anir, "we would have to send Elves with you, but I think that Peter and Sarah should stay behind."

He looked at the children. Peter was deep in thought, but Sarah looked back at Anir, almost angrily.

"I'm fed up with all this," she said, "I want to go home!"

"Well, perhaps you might be able to go," Anir replied, calmly. "At any rate, Gwyn wishes to see you all before he leaves and he will want to know what you have decided. I will leave you for a while to talk over what I have said."

And he rose from the stool and slipped silently away.

They did not begin to discuss anything straightaway. Each sat with their own thoughts for quite a little while. Then Sarah said:

"I want to go with you, Aunt Myf. I want to play on the beach again."

"But what about me?" retorted Peter, "It seems I can't take a step out of here without some witch or demon wanting to cast a spell on me! I want to get back to our holiday too, but it looks as though I'm stuck with all this. I think I shall get rid of my stone collection and collect stamps!"

Peter's voice became much raised by the end of this speech and he positively glared at Sarah.

"Now then, children PLEASE!" Aunt Myf had to almost shout at them. "Don't have a fight here. I just couldn't stand it! And my dear little car gone too. I only had the M.O.T. done a couple of months ago. Very upsetting and annoying it is!"

"I really don't know how you can be so calm Aunty," said Peter. "Supposing I'm sill stuck here when Mother and Father return to collect us after the University Summer School has finished?"

"We shall just have to cross that bridge when we come to it," said Aunt Myf, with just a hint of being annoyed.

They all sat silent again.

"It seems to me that Fate will decide this for us," said Aunt Myf at last, "I have got to go home and clear up or the Police will think I have been kidnapped, or worse. Sarah could come with me. This Orddu can have no interest in her. It is you Peter that they are after. They want you and that Stone."

"But, Aunt Myf," stammered Peter, "surely I can come home too? The Stone is here."

"I think you will have to ask Gwyn-ap-Nudd, he's bound to know. After all, he has been fighting these monsters for centuries! Now you two run along. I'm going to have a rest."

Aunt Myf settled herself on the bed and shut her eyes.

"Come on," said Peter, "let's go and wait for those Elves to finish eating."

"Where shall we go?"

"We'll go and sit in that golden room again. I want to think."

And with that Peter started down the labyrinth of passages again to find the golden throne room, which held the magic Stone.

As they passed the dining hall, they heard sounds of a meal being taken in almost sombre silence.

The Elves apparently were also in serious mood. Arddu, The Dark One, was a serious matter. At last they came to the huge wooden doors. Peter pushed on them and they opened, swinging back silently, to reveal the golden room.

"You know, at first, I thought the Elves preferred silver. They certainly seem to for everyday things."

"I know what you mean. But, hang on; of course!" cried Peter, "that is why our ancestors sometimes called this place Golden Hill."

"Clever old thing," said Sarah, slapping him on the back.

Their quarrels forgotten, they went to sit on the steps again. Somehow the peace of the room calmed the children as they pondered events.

"I think you ought to stay here with me, Sis," said Peter.

"But what about Aunt Myf, the break-in? There's bound to be an awful lot of clearing up to do. Someone ought to help her."

"Yes, there is that, I suppose," Peter sighed.

In his bones he felt that Sarah returning to the world outside with Aunt Myf was a very bad idea. He felt safe inside Arx Emain and was beginning to enjoy the strange way of life that the Elves had underground. Also, in an odd way, he felt that he must stay close to the Stone of Gardar, though why that should be, he did not know.

Their discussion over the 'pro's and con's' of Sarah's return, or not, with Aunt Myf went to and fro, until Anir's head appeared round the door.

"Come on, Peter, Sarah, The Lord Gwyn-ap-Nudd commands your presence in the Great Hall. I hope you have decided on your course of action."

"Er, not exactly," Sarah blushed.

She had begun to feel ashamed of her earlier remarks. Wishing to return to normal holiday life now struck her as rather selfish, under the circumstances. However, she was genuinely in a quandary as to what she ought to do. Aunt Myf would need help and the cronies of Arddu, Orddu and all of those could not possibly want her, or Aunty for anything at all; could they?

They arrived back in the Great Hall. The Elves had finished their meal. Gwyn-ap-Nudd was at the high table, still talking with some Elves, among whom were: Ederyn, Eldol and Aneryn.

With Aneryn was Aunt Myf. They were deep in plans and did not notice Peter, Sarah and Anir until they had climbed the stairs that led to the High Table.

"Welcome!" smiled the Lord Gwyn, and most surprisingly he arose and bowed to the children.

Peter bowed back and Sarah curtsied, it seemed the polite thing to do. Anir led round the table to Aunt Myf, who hugged them both tightly. He then went to stand behind Gwyn, who resumed his seat.

"Here we all are, then." Said Gwyn, "The armies will soon be gathered. And what shall your part be in all of this; Peter, Sarah, Myfanwy?"

He looked at each one of them in turn. It seemed to the children as if he were trying to read their thoughts.

"Spooky!" Sarah remarked afterwards.

"I at least must return, O Lord of the Fair People," said Aunt Myf.

"I agree," said Gwyn, "but what of the children? Are you happy to leave them here with Anir and Aneryn? They will be in safe hands, you have my word."

"I doubt it not," returned Aunt Myf " but I feel that I should have them with me."

"I do advise you, most seriously, to listen to the Lord Gwyn-ap-Nudd," broke in Anir, "my heart tells me that Arddu has good cause to fear Peter and the Stone, and he will seek to destroy them before they destroy him."

"Either that, or he will seek them to use them for his own dark purposes," said Gwyn, "after all, we speak of the Stone of Gardar. Peter has had time enough as its guardian to feel its power and may be able to wield it."

"Have you?" said Aneryn, sharply.

She suddenly looked hard at Peter; almost, as it were, straight through him. Peter frowned, thought for a while, then said quietly:

"Yes, I have."

"I felt it too, once, long ago," Aneryn said, laying her hand on his shoulder, "I know what it is."

Her hand was that of a young woman.

"Power!" said Gwyn, "All peoples lust after it."

"I will stay here," said Peter.

"I don't know what to do," wailed Sarah, miserably.

Her mind wrestled with the problem of how old Aneryn might be. She had forgotten, momentarily, that Elves are one of the Immortal Peoples.

"I don't know what I ought to do, but I want to go home," she wailed again.

"You come back with me then."

Aunt Myf patted and squeezed her hand kindly.

"It is decided," Gwyn-ap-Nudd said sternly, although he did not look happy, "but I am still of a mind to keep Sarah here with Peter."

Sarah was shaking her head.

"Very well. Anir, fetch Eldol back, he and the Lady Aneryn, Echel and Elivri must ride with Sarah and Myfanwy. Lady Aneryn, you know what to do and so do the others. Anir, you will stay here with the rest. I leave you in complete charge of my Halls, of Peter and the fate that rests in the Stone. You may not leave until I or, as is more likely Ederyn, return. Myfanwy, you and Sarah will go now while it is still daylight. A Guard will be posted around your dwelling to protect you from any further attack. I do not expect our enemies to return to your home, but do not even your army generals say: 'One must expect the unexpected'".

Gwyn sprang down from his seat as Eldol entered with two other Elves.

"The horses are ready, Lord," Eldol said, bowing low.

"With your permission, my Lord Gwyn, I will go and prepare myself for the journey," said the Lady Aneryn.

She almost ran down the steps of the dais and down the Great Hall.

"Why must we hurry?" asked Sarah, just as Anir returned with Eldol.

"Because, little lady, you must ride home before nightfall. The Dark One's power is greatest at night, as I have told you before!

It would not do to be out riding in the dark when his people are out and looking for you and Peter. At home you may lighten the darkness with many lamps. The Dark One's creatures do not love the light and you will be safe."

Anir looked out of breath and, Sarah thought, slightly irritated.

"Gwyn thinks as I do!" he looked at the Elf lord, who nodded assent from his throne, "We believe that having turned everything over in Myfanwy's house and found the Stone gone, they will have no further interest in the place. Now go and make ready. You ride soon!"

Aunt Myf and Sarah went with Peter to their rooms. They had brought nothing with them to Arx Emain, save themselves and the travel rug in which Peter had been wrapped when in the enchanted slumber. The rug now lay on Peter's bed.

They collected Sarah's jumper and Aunt Myf's cardigan. These had been cast off, as it was quite warm in Gwyn's underground domain. Then they said a rather tearful farewell to Peter.

"See you soon, take care of yourself my dear," said Aunt Myf, and hugged him close, "at least I know you will be safe here."

"Don't do anything silly," said Peter to Sarah.

"I'll try not to."

"Bye, then, Sarah."

"Bye, Peter."

Anir put his head round the door.

"You must come now. All is ready and the others are waiting."

"Good job I go pony trekking from time to time, isn't it?" Aunt Myf laughed.

Peter knew she was trying to make light of it all for his and Sarah's benefit. Good old Aunt Myf, just like her! He waved as they turned the corner into the passage that led to the front door. He then went and sat down miserably on his bed, feeling like a spare part and wondering what to do next.

Anir hurried Aunt Myf and Sarah off to, and out of, the front door. There they found Aneryn, mounted already upon a beautiful grey horse. Sarah was surprised to see that she was dressed like Anir, in breeches, tunic and cloak, instead of her graceful blue dress.

Three other Elves were with her: Eldol, Elivri and Echel were also mounted on their steeds, ready for the journey. Sarah climbed onto the pony that had been brought for her; a dear little skewbald, and Aunt Myf was soon seated more gingerly on a rather large brown horse. Sarah blinked in the sunshine. It was a lovely afternoon.

"Farewell!" said Anir, as the Elves began to encourage the horses into a walk, "And may the blessing of Gwyn-ap-Nudd, and all who dwell in Arx Emain, be with you."

"Farewell!" they called back. Eldol's beast broke into a trot and at last they were on their way back to Aunt Myf's home at Cwm-yr-Eglwys.

"Back home! I'm going home," chanted Sarah happily to herself, as her pony trotted merrily along.

Then she thought of Peter and felt rather guilty.

"This takes me back to when I was a girl," trilled Aunt Myf cheerily from atop her horse, "I used to muck out at the local stables and then I used to get a free ride. Come on Sarah, we shall soon get home at this rate."

They crossed the main road.

"How far is it from here?" asked Sarah.

"About seven or eight miles as the crow flies," Eldol told her, "never fear, we shall be back before it is truly dark."

And he spurred his horse into a canter. Somehow Sarah's pony had difficulty in cantering and most of the time did a cross between a very fast trot and a canter.

The terrain was awkward. Ascending a hill was not too bad, it was the descending that was the trouble. The horses would trot down the hills and Sarah's pony insisted upon putting its neck out and its head down. Sarah felt that eventually she might 'bump, bump,' down its neck, as on a slide, until she slid off altogether. Of course she did not do anything of the sort, it just felt like it.

They hurried over the main road near Fishguard, well after what ought to have been teatime; indeed, it was probably nearer to Sarah's suppertime. Eldol took them speedily on round the outskirts of the town. The roads were quiet; probably everyone was home for the evening. And it was a beautiful summer's evening.

As they crossed a bridge over the river Gwaun, midges rose in clouds above the water and house martins swooped overhead, making the most of the abundant insect life. The sun was beginning its descent into the sea beyond. The seals would be playing in the bay below Aunt Myf's cottage, thought Sarah, wistfully.

The riders came to the coast road. Eldol looked up and down the road and from side to side. He particularly cast his gaze at the hills, which rise up from the coast and lead, at last, to the Prescelly range.

"There is no sign of Orddu or of any of the Dark One's creatures. I do not feel any evil presence either, so I will risk our riding on the road itself."

"Will the motorists see us?" asked Aunt Myf.

"They may indeed," replied Eldol, "but they will think they have seen a few holidaymakers out late after a pleasant trek."

"It doesn't feel very pleasant!" thought Sarah to herself, "Are we nearly there yet?"

"About two or three miles at most," said Eldol.

"Come, ride by me, little maid," Aneryn said, smiling, "we will finish this journey together."

And, setting her horse next to Sarah's pony, she ensured that they kept pace with each other.

Aunt Myf, who was eager to see what had befallen her property, went on in haste with the other Elves. So at last they turned left down the track that led from the road to Aunt Myf's house.

When Sarah and Aneryn arrived at the front porch, they were surprised to find a very red faced Aunt Myf in animated conversation with the local policeman. Aneryn and Sarah dismounted and went to join her. Eldol, Elivri and Echel had obviously bade farewell, as they were mounting ready to leave.

Eldol waved to Aneryn who pushed Sarah towards Aunt Myf and went over to him.

"I shall stay here awhile," he said, "then it will be Echel's turn to be on guard, then Elivri. If all remains well with Sarah and the Aunt you may return with him to Arx Emain at the end of his turn."

Aneryn turned to the others:

"Good speed," she said.

They were on the point of leaving, when Sarah ran up to them.

"Wait!" she cried, "Can't you take some things back with you for Peter? Goodness knows how long he may be stuck in your tunnels. Not that they aren't very, very nice tunnels," she added as an afterthought, "but your Elvish way of life is so different to ours."

Then, before anyone could say anything, Sarah ran past Aunt Myf and Sergeant Emmanuel and into the house. This was easily done, for the front door had been broken down and now swung lopsided on its hinges.

What a sight met her eyes! All was turned out and turned over. It was easy to see why Sergeant Emmanuel had been on door duty. Sarah ran into Peter's room. Here was the worst mess of all.

However, in the corner, behind a beanbag was the cache of Peter's favourite books kept for rainy days.

These were undisturbed, so Sarah snatched them up and looked for some spare clothes. These were scattered all over the floor where drawers had been emptied. She ran back to Eldol with a supermarket bag full of goodies, including the battered teddy that no one must ever know about. She thrust the bag at Eldol.

"Give these to Peter. They are very important," she said.

Eldol bowed as well as he could in the saddle.

"Peter shall have these as soon as I return to Arx Emain, before I have given my full report to Anir!" he smiled and bowed again, "Farewell, we shall meet again 'ere long."

"Goodbye," said Sarah.

"Goodbye," called Aneryn and Aunt Myf.

Sergeant Emmanuel was writing in his notebook.

"Went off on pony trek -- returned to find house burgled. Sergeant Emmanuel on duty, having been called to the scene of the crime earlier today by Mr. Evans the milkman. Today being the second of August."

He licked his pencil and cleared his throat.

"You had better go in and see if there has been much stolen, Myfanwy," he said, and ushered her in through the broken door.

Sarah and Aneryn followed.

"I'll put the kettle on for tea, Aunty," said Sarah and went with Aneryn to the kitchen.

Fortunately there was little damage in this room and they busied themselves preparing a supper with what food there was available. Aunt Myf all the while making pretence at looking to see if anything was stolen. When at last she could not suggest anything to Sergeant Emmanuel, she invited him to take tea, but he would not.

"No, no, indeed my other half is waiting with my dinner at home and she will be very annoyed if I get in too late. Thanks, Myfanwy, maybe another time, perhaps tomorrow. We shall have to have a full statement. I will come at half past ten. That will give you time to clear up. A very strange business altogether! Good night all."

He tipped his cap and stepped out into the night. They heard his bicycle tyres crunching up the drive.

"Thank goodness! Now we can have something to eat," said Aunt Myf.

They were soon seated round the kitchen table and there was silence for quite some time after that.

Later, after the washing up, Sarah had a hot bath and climbed thankfully into bed. She fell into a deep sleep. Far away, in the house of Gwyn-ap-Nudd, Peter had done the same, having remained wakeful only long enough to make sure that the 'pony trekkers' had not returned.

He had hoped so much that they would, but eventually Morvith, who had tended him before came to beg him to go to sleep. She was quite right to do so, as it turned out. Eldol and Elivri did not arrive until dawn. They had had several unpleasant adventures upon the way and were discussing them with Anir when Peter came, bleary eyed, into the Great Hall.

He went to get himself some breakfast, then went over to the group and sat on the floor behind Eldol. Immediately, Eldol rose and handed to him the supermarket bag that Sarah had filled with his things. Anir turned towards him;

"Eldol brings these to you, they are from your sister."

"Oh thank you, Eldol, thank you!" said Peter seizing the bag greedily.

He had come to enjoy being with the Elves but one can have too much of a good thing. Sarah had sent him his most favourite things.

He peeped into the bag. It contained books, a few spare clothes, his wash bag and other necessities, including the teddy bear that must never be mentioned.

The Elves returned to their conversation with Anir. A tear started in Peter's eye as he looked at the things that Sarah had sent. He could not help himself. Suddenly he felt he could run straight out of Arx Emain and back home. Instead he slunk out of the Hall and went down the corridor to the room where the Stone was kept.

He pushed the doors open and took his belongings to the foot of the dais, upon which rested the golden throne of Gwyn-ap-Nudd. Peter started to read one of his books in the glow of the Stone. One and half hours later, Anir found him.

"I am very glad to find you at last," he said, "time must hang heavy when you are not active on Elvish business and away from your loved ones."

"Yes," said Peter slowly, "I wonder what Sarah is doing now? I do wish she had stayed."

"By Eldol's account, she and your Aunt have a great deal to do at the cottage. But do not fear; they are safe. Aneryn and others are guarding them. You are safe too, as long as you are here."

"I just wish that there was something that I could do."

"You are helping our cause very greatly by remaining here with the Stone," sighed Anir, looking up at the Stone in its niche.

The glow from it never wavered. Anir spoke again:

"Here, in Arx Emain it is in its rightful place. Gwyn and the Elves will not use its full power except in the very greatest of dire need."

Anir came to the dais and sat down beside Peter. Peter realised that Anir was in a good listening mood.

"But," said he," why must I stay with the Stone if it is safe here?"

Anir looked at Peter sympathetically.

"Anyone who has kept the Stone for any length of time as you did becomes 'in tune' with its power. It has a very great magic within it. The Elves know how to use it, but so does Arddu, or thinks he does. He thinks that he might be able to bend its power to do his evil will. I think that he is mistaken, but the Elves dare not take the risk."

Anir rose to go.

"But me!" cried Peter, "What about me?"

Anir looked down at him kindly.

"You kept the Stone for a long time, as these things go," he said softly, "you too could use it."

"Me!" Peter stared at Anir in disbelief, "but how? I don't know how, I wouldn't, couldn't know..." he stammered.

"If the time should come," Anir said solemnly, "the Stone itself would guide you. You would be shown what to do and you could bring the power of the Samildanach down upon whomsoever you wished. That is why Arddu wants you because you are a danger to him. However, you are also a danger to the Elves because Arddu might try to capture you and force you to use the Stone against us. That is what Gwyn-ap-Nudd has said. Personally, I do not think that Arddu could force the power of the Samildanach to work against the Elves. It would be like using their very own power against themselves. That is what I think, but I may be wrong. Who knows? Gwyn-ap-Nudd possibly, but he is not here. A few days and he will be returning from over the sea with his kinsfolk. We must wait for his call. Ederyn will join us with armies from the north; then we must ride to the meeting place where all the Elves will gather for battle!"

"Then must I stay here all the time?"

Peter looked wistfully at Anir. The thought occurred to him that he would actually rather enjoy meeting the Elvish armies.

"For the present you must stay. But," Anir paused, he saw the disappointment in Peter's eyes, "and a BIG but it is too -- we will only know the answers to that and many other questions when Gwyn-ap-Nudd has gathered all his armies and sent messengers to tell us what passes. That may take time, perhaps a week, perhaps longer. But do not be afraid, you may not have to wait too long and then you will be free to go."

"Oh, I do hope so," said Peter.

Anir patted him on the head. Peter rather resented this. Then Anir strode out of the room and Peter picked up his belongings and followed. Anir returned down the corridor towards the Great Hall.

"More plans afoot," thought Peter, and took himself off back to his room.

"If only," he thought, for about the millionth time, "Mother and Father were not both at the University Summer School again this year!"

He felt that his parents would not stand for any of this present nonsense, or would they? Were they like Aunt Myf? She was different. She was in league with the Elves! A very strange sort of Grown-up. Being a member of the Celtic History Society obviously did you no good at all.

CHAPTER FIVE

More Trouble With Orddu

That night, Peter fell sleepily into bed, having had an excellent dinner, a surfeit of Elvish stories and songs, AND a final 'goodnight story' from Morvith about the Olden Days.

She had regaled him with the events that used to take place during the Spring Festivals in the mountains. Meanwhile, Sarah was already in bed and fast asleep. She had had a very tiring day helping Aunt Myf set the cottage to rights again.

After supper she had taken time off to go to the Point, where she watched the seals playing round the rocks until the sun began to go down. Aneryn had come to find her and beg her to come inside before nightfall. Sarah, having no desire to meet with any of Orddu's creatures, almost ran back.

"I will watch you whenever you come out here on your own. You must not be here alone. Until our people have put Arddu in his place, you are not safe. In fact, I think you really ought to have stayed in Arx Emain with your brother."

Sarah flushed, she felt guilty now she was here, at leaving Peter behind.

"Someone had to help Aunt Myf," she began.

"Yes, but I wonder also if your Aunt should be here either. Never mind, in you go, and keep safe. If danger threatens, you will both have to return to Arx Emain and we will have to think of an excuse to give to your Aunt's neighbours and to Sergeant Emmanuel!"

"Goodnight, then," said Sarah, and passed into the cottage. Aunt Myf had made a very good supper and they were both glad to retire early for the night, having first locked a brand new front door and all the windows.

The night passed uneventfully, and the next day and the day after that. In fact nothing remarkable occurred for some time so that Sarah was lulled into the false sense of thinking that nothing was going to happen until Gwyn-ap-Nudd's armies beat Arddu in battle. Then dawned a day when all seemed more than usually perfect.

The morning began bright and sun filled. Sarah woke feeling as if the events of days past must have been a dream, save for the fact that Peter was not there. Even Aunt Myf seemed quite cheery.

"How many eggs, dear?" she asked; giving Sarah a beaming smile from over the laden frying pan, where bacon and sausages already lay sizzling.

"Oh, two please," said Sarah, and set about laying the table.

Through the window the sea glittered in the distance. The day promised to be hot!

"May I go to the beach today, please, please, can I?

Aunt Myf's face clouded for a moment.

"Well," she said slowly, in a considering sort of way, "I suppose we do have our protectors."

"It would be such a pity to miss the weather and the seals were playing last night. I'll only go for the morning and be back for lunch."

Sarah's eyes pleaded her case.

"All right, then," Aunt Myf said at length, "but come straight back here at twelve o'clock. That way I shan't worry. I still have some cleaning and tidying to do, and about two tons of ironing."

"Great! Thanks Aunt Myf."

Sarah pushed her empty breakfast plate from her, kissed Aunt Myf and flew to her room, breakfast tea mug in hand. She soon made up a bundle containing swimming gear, towel and sun lotion (UV factor 20, just in case -- Aunt Myf was always safety conscious). She also took a book, a hat and sunglasses.

Draining her mug of tea to the dregs, Sarah rushed out via the kitchen, from which she collected a banana and two chocolate biscuits.

"Oh! I see there are going to be *penguins* on our beach this morning," said Aunt Myf.

"Ha! Ha! Very funny, Aunty; see you later alligator, bye!" and Sarah was gone.

Aunt Myf smiled and turned to the washing up and then to the ironing.

"A nice quiet morning's work I shall have and then tea in the garden," she thought pleasantly to herself, "I'll mow the grass and we can have a nice cream tea and sit on the lawn."

She turned on the radio and began to iron T-shirts. Mozart's Clarinet Concerto floated over the ether.

"Such a calming melody," Aunt Myf said to herself.

On the beach Sarah had spread her towel. The sun had warmed sea and sand and she stretched herself out on her stomach, hat pulled down and sleepily sorted out a few pretty shells from the sand. She must have dozed for a few minutes as she started up with a feeling that her hands were wet, as indeed they were.

The incoming tide had caught her and most of her front and the towel were wet. The water was pleasantly cool. Having moved towel and belongings to a drier haven, further up the beach, Sarah plunged into the blue waves.

Round the corner, the seals were playing, and the whole world seemed to be playing with them. Seagulls swooped overhead and it appeared to Sarah that the little bay had never looked so pretty.

Near midday, as Sarah dried herself off on the beach, Aunt Myf was getting a little lunch ready. Sarah must come back soon.

"I'll just go and pick some fresh mint for the dressing," she thought, and went out into the garden to fetch it.

Sarah packed up her things, tilted the sun hat forwards on her head, slung her beach bag over her shoulder and began to climb up the path that led back to Aunt Myf's cottage. When she arrived, the back door was open. In the kitchen a very nice lunch was laid out on the table: ham, salad and potato salad.

"Aunt Myf, I'm back," Sarah called happily.

There was no reply. Perhaps she had gone to her room and didn't hear. Sarah looked in the bedroom, then the bathroom and then through the cottage. Aunt Myf was nowhere to be seen.

"Oh where has she gone?" fussed Sarah, angry now because she had enjoyed her morning on the beach.

By this time she was feeling very hungry. She also felt that this hiccup threatened to spoil the nice ' normal' time she was having.

"Bother Aunt Myf! Well, I'll just eat some lunch before I look anymore. Anyway, she'll probably turn up if I start without her. She must have forgotten something and popped up to the corner shop."

Sarah gave herself a large helping of potato salad and tried to make herself feel comfortable about eating lunch alone, but it was not fun. She ate quickly and being careful to leave a good portion for Aunt Myf, she put her dishes in the sink and took an apple to eat for dessert.

Aunt Myf still refused to appear, so she covered the rest of lunch with plastic film and put it in the fridge. Then taking a can of 'cola' and another apple, she went to make a search of the garden and paths.

Far away in Arx Emain, Peter had become fed up with reading and Stone watching. This particular afternoon, after a very large luncheon, he had taken a nap in his room. He woke suddenly at three o'clock, after an uneasy dream in which he had somehow been employed at rescuing gerbils from the tops of trees! (Sarah and he had once had a pair of pale fawn gerbils).

He had just handed the penultimate gerbil to Sarah, who was standing on a ladder below him, when something made him jump. Rubbing the sleep from his eyes, he pulled himself together and ran down the corridor to find Anir, Aneryn Morvith, ANYONE! Deep in his heart something told that Sarah and Aunt Myf were in danger.

At three o'clock Sarah had stopped searching and was sitting on the garden wall in front of the cottage, wondering what to do next. Should she go and telephone Sergeant Emmanuel? Should she try and find Aneryn and the Elf guard in the woods?

She had just decided upon the former course of action and had jumped down from the wall in preparation for return to the cottage, when Aneryn found her. She ran from the woods above the cottage, looking about her from side to side, in a state of great anxiety.

"Sarah, Sarah, you must come with me quickly. Please come and help, I have just found your Aunt."

"What's happened? Aunt Myf?"

"We have just found her, Echel and I, as we were making a patrol around the cottage. I am not certain, but I think she has felt the breath of Orddu."

"Oh no!" cried Sarah, and she began to cry.

Aneryn patted her hand and pulled her over towards the wood.

"Come on, help us to get her into the cottage."

As she spoke, she pulled Sarah towards the woods. They ran forward. Just as the undergrowth began to grow sparse under the trees, Sarah saw Aunt Myf lying face down on the leaves. Was she alive or was she...?

Aneryn motioned Sarah to help turn her. When they got her face up, Aunt Myf gave a strange snort.

"Thank goodness!" thought Sarah.

Then with another snort came a twisted smile, as if she were in some kind of enchanted dream. Aunt Myf then opened her eyes, smiled at Sarah and said:

"I am Bloddwen's...!"

"Bloddwen's what?" demanded Sarah, urgently.

"I am Bloddwen's...!"

"She is not finishing the sentence," complained Sarah.

"What on earth is she talking about?"

Aunt Myf shut her eyes.

"I think I could make a guess," said Aneryn, "but it is only a guess and can wait until I see Anir in Arx Emain."

"Yes," she said, watching Sarah's face fall, "we must return with the greatest haste. Ah! Here is Echel with the horses."

Echel appeared through the trees with two horses, much to Sarah's disappointment. He bowed low to Aneryn.

"My lady Aneryn," he said softly, "there are about a half dozen of Orddu's creatures to the north of the road. There are but seven hours of clear daylight remaining to us. How shall we manage to gain Arx Emain before it is truly dark and the creatures of Orddu become a serious threat?"

"Let us get this poor lady to her cottage while we think."

"Very well my Lady, but we had best think quickly."

Echel and Aneryn made a cradle under Aunt Myf's head and chest and motioned Sarah to carry her feet. Gently they got her into the cottage and put her down on the sofa.

"This is bad," said Echel, "we are only three. Elivri was not due here until tomorrow night."

"It is very serious," agreed Aneryn, "but we must be in Arx Emain again, somehow, before midnight. We cannot withstand a full attack here. If the creatures are near, Orddu cannot be far away. I do not understand. Something is going on in this area that must be part of the larger plan Arddu has, concerning Gwyn and the Stone."

Sarah suddenly had a brainwave.

"If we could get Aunt Myf to walk, I know how we can get nearly to Arx Emain in half an hour. And Echel, you could meet us by the road!"

Aunt Myf opened her eyes again.

"I am Bloddwen's..." she sighed.

Sarah patted her hair.

"All right Aunty, come on, wake up, please do!" she whispered softly in her ear.

Surprisingly, Aunt Myf did seem to waken just a little. She opened her eyes wider and sat up.

"I am Bloddwen's...!"

"If only she could walk, I can get her almost to Arx Emain" repeated Sarah.

"How?" queried Aneryn.

"There's a BUS STOP opposite the track to Arx Emain. It's a request stop for the bus that goes to Haverfordwest. If Aunty will walk to the bus stop in the village we can go on the bus."

"But surely you will not manage her in this state?" said Echel.

"Well, Sarah may be right. However, she will certainly need assistance and I have never ridden in one of your 'horseless carriages'," mused Aneryn, "would your 'BUS' also carry me?" she asked.

"Of course!" cried Sarah. Then a thought struck her.

"Suppose Sergeant Emanuel comes back? I'd better have some explanation as to why we are away. Let's think: Um, Er, we've done the 'pony trekking' one, what can we say?"

She sat down to think, head in hands.

"I know she said at last, I'll ring Sergeant Emmanuel and tell him that we're going to Skomer Island to do some bird watching. People often do stay on there you know. I'll also ask him to keep an eye on the cottage."

And with that, she rushed off to the 'phone.

"I am Bloddwen's...!" said Aunt Myf.

When Sarah returned she was smiling.

"Well, that's fixed. Now then, there's a bus at half past four which will get us to Arx Emain, or nearly so, by five."

"I will need some disguise," said Aneryn, "people will be able to see me on the bus. It would look rather odd if one of your companions were invisible. Therefore I shall wish myself to be seen, but I had better not look too strange."

"I've thought of that," replied Sarah, and she disappeared to Aunty's bedroom.

"I shall, with your leave, ride to the appointed place and meet you with horses. Guards will be posted near to the Hill of our Kingdom and I can get help from them and raise the alarm if you deem it necessary," said Echel.

"I deem it so. Let it be done as you say."

Aneryn and Echel bowed to each other and soon afterwards, Echel could be seen riding lie the wind, away from the cottage, closely followed by Aneryn's horse.

Sarah returned with an old crochet cardigan of Aunt Myf's and a large sun hat of Italian straw, which had seen better days. A few battered roses hung from a faded green ribbon round it. She also carried one of Aunt Myf's old handbags. She proffered the 'disguise' to Aneryn.

"Here, you don't have to put anything in the bag," she said, "just carry it and wear these and you'll look almost normal."

Aneryn put the cardigan over the long grey tunic she was wearing.

"Don't worry about your long skirt, they can be quite fashionable these days."

Sarah ran off again. She went to fetch a few items from her and Peter's rooms and then made ready to lock up the cottage.

"We had better leave," said Aneryn.

"Come on Aunt Myf, I do hope you can walk."

"I am Bloddwen's...!" said Aunt Myf flatly.

Sarah pulled her arm and with Aneryn's help got her to stand up.

"Walk, Aunty, please walk!" said Sarah.

"I am Bloddwen's...!"

"Come ON Aunt Myf!" Sarah raised her voice.

It seemed to work, for Aunt Myf began to walk to the door.

"Good!" said Aneryn.

When Aunt Myf reached the front door Aneryn stood behind her and put her hands on Aunt Myf's head and whispered something to her. After that, they had not much difficulty in setting Aunt Myf to go where they wanted her to go.

Sarah locked the front door behind them and the three of them started off up the track towards the village and the bus stop.

"And a motley three we look, too!" thought Sarah.

Meanwhile, Peter was trying to explain to Anir and the Elves what he felt.

"Calm yourself, please, little man," said Eldol, as Peter began to dance up and down with vexation.

Peter ignored the 'little man' description of himself, and spoke up passionately:

"But something is wrong. I can feel it."

Anir came late into the Great Hall and Peter had to tell his story once again.

"Come Peter, sit down, take a good breath and explain to us what you think is happening."

"I was asleep. I woke up and all of a sudden, it was as if someone had called me, just like when we get called for school in the mornings at home. So I got up and I just felt inside of me a feeling that something is wrong, perhaps with Sarah and Aunt Myf. I don't know, but it's coming to me stronger every minute."

He looked round the Hall, as if Arddu and all his dark army would come crawling through the walls at any moment. Eldol looked at Anir and they nodded at each other.

"Double the guards outside and extra on the gates," said Eldol, grimly.

He signed to a tall Elf at the doorway who bowed low and disappeared in a hurry. Peter was very surprised. He had expected to have a lengthy argument with those in charge of Arx Emain in order to persuade them to do anything at all. Again, as if Eldol read his thoughts, the Elf said to him:

"We thank you, Peter, and we take account of what you say, for you are sensitive to many things having handled The Gardar

Stone. This may be the first move of Arddu's against us. He will know from his spies that Gwyn and Ederyn have not yet gathered all their armies together. He is probably preparing to strike a blow early, hoping to catch us off guard, thereby winning some advantage. He will attempt to confuse us also with his wiles. He little knows how ready we are! However, some trickery he may have planned that was not in our calculations and we must be ready for that also."

Turning to Anir he said:

"I suggest we post messengers from here to the cottage at Cwm-yr-Eglwys. If an attack is made upon Peter's relations then the guards themselves may need assistance."

"Aye, my lord Eldol," said Anir, "but suppose the enemy has them already?"

"Then we take council and think again. You mortals must always rush into everything! Do not climb the mountain until it sits in your path."

Eldol turned to Peter who, ashen white, sat on the bench beside Anir.

"Morvith, bring us some water please. This young gentleman looks as if he might faint."

"I will not!" said Peter, most vehemently.

But he was pleased to drink a mug of water when Morvith brought it.

"May I emphasise to you, Peter," said Anir, "that you must not leave Arx Emain just now for any reason. I mean that even if your family should ask or even if you thought it would save a life, you must not go! Do I make myself perfectly clear?"

"Yes sir!" said Peter, more astonished than ever.

"Just in case," said Eldol, looking hard at Peter, "it were wise to put a guard at Peter's door also."

"Don't you trust me?" asked Peter, worried.

He was an honest boy and to have people, or Elves believing him to be untrustworthy was something he found deeply shocking.

"We trust you, never fear, but we do not trust The Dark One. He plays many tricks to get what he wants. That is the power he wields in the world."

"But I don't see why I should have a guard. Arddu can't get inside Arx Emain can he?"

Eldol smiled:

"He cannot come inside Arx Emain, not even with Gwyn away. Also we have the power of the Stone to protect us. No I do not fear that."

"Well then, what?" Peter's eyebrows shot upwards.

He could not follow the Elf's reasoning at all.

"Do you not see, Peter," broke in Anir, "you may be the key that Arddu requires to unlock the power of the Stone. He cannot come in here to take it -- and you!"

Here Peter turned pale again.

"But he might, by his evil arts, tempt you in a dream to come out to him bringing the Stone with you. Thus he would gain the Stone and someone to wield it for him."

"Oh, goodness! I never thought he could do that."

Peter had so far felt himself completely safe inside the Elf Kingdom. This last was a shock to him.

"I have explained some of the dangers to you before," said Anir seriously, "but as long as you do not leave here you are fairly safe. However, your sister and Aunt are now of some concern. We will do all in our power to see that they are safe, so do not think of going out to help them yourself. You must be very strong, Peter, although the temptation to leave may become overpowering, you must not give in. It is of Arddu's making."

"Yet I say this," said Eldol suddenly, "if you are determined to resist temptation, you will receive help."

"Thank you," said Peter quietly.

He knew that now he was really the Elves' prisoner, even if they did not put it quite like that. There was nothing he could do. Sarah and Aunt Myf could be in danger and he was unable to do a thing to help them. He buried his head in his hands.

"Come and sit by me," said Morvith, "we will be setting supper out shortly and there will be a tale and some singing after, which may cheer you up a little."

"Very well, I will," said Peter.

Then he called out to Anir who had got up to leave with Eldol.

"Hey, Anir," Anir looked round, "please, can you tell me: how long will Gwyn be away?"

"Do you not recall? Two days, maybe three to go over the sea. Then he has to gather the kindred together and bring them back to the meeting place. From tomorrow onwards we shall be waiting for his messengers. Perhaps Ederyn will return first. He will bring Elves from the North kingdom, which is very powerful. Now I have business with Eldol and some of the others. We must set a new guard and make plans in case Arddu does think that he can attack us. Farewell."

And with that he left the Hall.

Peter went and sat miserably on a stool by the fire. Morvith and others were busy bringing in food for the evening feast. It always was a feast here in Arx Emain. True this place was wonderful, beautiful beyond anything he had ever seen in the world outside, but he longed to see the sky once more and walk on the grass under the trees. Even to have Sarah tease him again, like she always did, would be preferable to being a prisoner in this Elvish paradise.

A great longing for the world outside, the REAL world, welled up in him. It was so strong that he nearly ran out of the Elf Kingdom there and then, risking all. What was happening outside? Where were Sarah and Aunt Myf? He threw a twig angrily onto the fire and watched it crackle and burn.

"Do not let the Destroyer influence your head or your heart," said a voice.

It was Morvith. She brought Peter a dish of vegetable broth and some crusty bread. Then she sat beside him while he ate. She remained silent until he had finished.

"Do not worry, Peter, your people will come to you soon. I know it, I feel it."

"Thank you Morvith."

Morvith removed Peter's dishes.

"Listen to the singing and be cheered." she said, and went to join the other Elves.

Peter did as Morvith bade him. In fact he had not much choice, but after she spoke to him he had begun to feel just a little better. Perhaps Sarah and Aunt Myf were on their way to join him. Perhaps at any moment they would arrive.

He was waiting for something positive. This was much better than all the doom and gloom that he had had from Anir about Arddu coming to get him. Peter shuddered and thought to himself:

"I will concentrate on Sarah. I do so wish that she would come soon."

At Cwm-yr-Eglwys a strange trio waited at the bus stop in the village. There was a stop slightly nearer but Aneryn had asked if there was one nearer to 'the houses of men' and advised waiting there instead.

"I doubt Orddu or her creatures would dare attack three of us in daylight and so near to the ordinary Menfolk of your village."

"I jolly well hope you're right," said Sarah, and meant it!

The bus arrived almost on time. Actually it was five minutes late but at four thirty five they were climbing onto the bus. Sarah paid for all of them out of Aunt Myf's housekeeping purse and sat

Aneryn in the middle of the bus. Then, having collected the tickets, she went to sit behind them.

"I am Bloddwen's...!" said Aunt Myf, for about the 2000th time!

Thought Sarah:

"This is beginning to be really irritating."

She looked at Aneryn who sat close to Aunt Myf on the inside of the seat. Her head tilted forwards so that the straw hat had almost covered her face. The bus roared on its way. Aneryn spoke never a word.

"I wonder if she is nervous, being on a bus for the first time," Sarah wondered to herself.

With Aunt Myf deep in an enchanted trance and the Elf lady silent, for whatever reason, Sarah had time to think over events. She suddenly, desperately wished that Peter were there. What a beastly selfish person she had been. She felt sorry that she had wanted her holiday, no THEIR holiday back to normal again. The Elves were right, she should have stayed with Peter at Arx Emain. If only she had, perhaps Aunt Myf would not be in this state. This day, which had started off so well for her, had ended in near calamity. Sarah gave herself a good telling off.

"You should have waited at Arx Emain, like they said. Only two or three days and Gwyn might be back from over the sea and Ederyn returned from the North Kingdom. Perhaps," she mused, "I wonder if they have any news at Arx Emain. I expect Peter will be one of the first to know."

That set Sarah off thinking about her brother and how callously she had used him. Involuntarily, a large tear dripped from her right eye and plopped on her knee. She took out a tissue, blew her nose and tried to compose herself. Sarah was so dispirited that she did not notice dark shadows moving in the trees by the roadside.

"I am Bloddwen's..., I am Bloddwen's...!" cried Aunt Myf, in a very agitated fashion.

"All right, all right, calm down now Aunt Myf. We shall soon be there and everything will be all right!"

Aunt Myf's agitated state had brought Sarah out of herself. The bus sped on its way. Soon she must get up and press the bell so that it would stop at the request stop.

"Oh I do hope Echel has arrived. Oh please let him be there," whispered Sarah, under her breath.

She rose and pressed the bell. The bus drew to a halt and let the three of them off. To the left of the bus stop in a small spinney of ash trees Echel was walking a sweating horse up and down.

As soon as she alighted from the bus, Aneryn spied Echel and she ran to him.

"Ah! Well met brother Elf," she cried.

"Well met indeed!" replied Echel "There are a great many of Orddu's creatures about to the north and the east."

"Yes, I saw them as I traveled inside the human's horseless carriage. A useful machine, but I must say that a journey on one is not something that I should care to repeat. Nasty, noisy smelly thing!"

"Come on Aunty" Sarah was saying, as she pulled Aunt Myf towards the Elves' meeting place.

"She had better ride. I think my horse will stand the path to Arx Emain now," said Echel.

"My horse Wen, Did she follow?" asked Aneryn.

"Aye, Lady, but not as swift as I rode for I knew I must be here to meet you."

Echel turned to Sarah and Aunt Myf.

"Haste, haste! Come Ladies, both of you must mount."

Echel led his horse around to where Aunt Myf stood transfixed, staring into nothingness. Sarah prepared herself to assist the Elves in getting Aunt Myf up onto Echel's steed. They had just all got hold of her, when they heard the noise of horse's hooves on the road behind them.

Echel threw back the cloak he was wearing to reveal the short blade he was carrying, though it was more of a long knife than a sword. Quickly he drew it and rushed towards the sound.

"Orddu and her creatures! And yet, maybe?"

Aneryn stood in front of Aunt Myf to protect her.

"Get behind me Sarah until we see who comes."

Suddenly the horse and its rider appeared; crashing through the bushes as they made their way from the road to Arx Emain. Echel ran back to the little group. He was grinning from ear to ear.

"It is the Lord Ederyn. He is come at last!"

"Well, I didn't think it was the enemy with you rushing back like that!" muttered Sarah, under her breath, as Ederyn's horse plunged through the undergrowth and came into view.

"Welcome, welcome," cried Aneryn and ran to greet Ederyn.

However, although Ederyn smiled back at her and Echel, it was a grim smile.

"No time have I to greet you as I should."

He drew his horse up beside Sarah, reined in and dismounted.

"The armies of the Northern Kindreds are approaching Arx Emain. I have ridden on ahead of them and I have been followed this last mile by a THING that is grey and wolf-like."

He looked at Aunt Myf. One look told him all. He made a sign to Echel and almost in one move, together they lifted Aunt Myf up on to Echel's horse; and before she knew what was happening; Sarah was being lifted by Aneryn, up behind Ederyn.

Echel with Aunt Myf were already riding as fast as they could away to the entrance of the Elf Kingdom. A horse that had to be Aneryn's trotted into the spinney. Sarah saw her mount.

"We follow!" she heard Aneryn call, as with a mighty bound, Ederyn sped away from the spinney and on to Arx Emain.

"Hold tight Sarah! No, tighter still, little maid," Ederyn called to her.

Sarah held on as best she could. Then something made her hang on like 'grim death'. Out of the corner of her eye she saw something that looked like a very large dog. It was a huge grey she-wolf, though its shape was shadowy, like smoke. Fire flashed in its eyes, and worse still, others came in a massive crowd behind it. These wolves were smaller but no less terrifying.

"Don't look!" commanded Ederyn, as he spurred his horse on to greater speed.

Ash trees, birches and brambles flew past in a blur. Sarah shut her eyes but she was sure she could feel the giant wolf's breath on her leg. It seemed an eternity before she heard other voices.

"Elves," she thought, "Arx Emain. We've got there after all!"

Sarah heard the gates of the Elf kingdom open; the clatter as Ederyn's horse crossed the inner courtyard; the shouts of joyful welcome for the brother of Gwyn-ap-Nudd, King of the Elves. Only when she realised that Ederyn's horse had stopped and that she was being lifted from its back, did Sarah dare to open her eyes.

Aunt Myf had already been helped away to one of the underground rooms where Morvith and others were waiting to care for her. Ederyn was swamped by his kinsfolk who were eager for news. He was swept down the corridor with Echel and the Lady Aneryn, who had managed to escape the wolves, also by a hair's breadth.

Sarah watched them disappear towards the Great Hall. It seemed as if they had all forgotten about her. She was wondering what to do and where to go, when a voice whispered her name:

"Sarah."

It was Peter!

"Oh Peter!"

Peter came out from the pillar behind which he had been standing. He had been watching the arrival of the others. They hugged each other for a long time. Then Sarah said:

"I'm really sorry I left you."

"And I'm sorry that you have had all that trouble with Aunt Myf."

He patted her on the shoulder.

"It's time you had something to eat. Let's go! The others have gone to the Great Hall, come on, let's follow them. You look as if you could do with something."

"I certainly could," replied Sarah, "I've had rather a shock."

"I can tell you have," her brother said, sympathetically.

He led her down the dark tunnels to the Great Hall. It was now filled with candle light and light from the fire, and was decorated with early autumn and late summer fruits and flowers. Ederyn was seated at table to the right of Gwyn's throne. Next to him were Anir, Aneryn, Echel and their friends.

Morvith noticed the children's arrival and found them a place at table, having reassured them of Aunt Myf's condition, which was 'comfortable'.

"I've had something already," said Peter, "you dig in. You can tell me your news when you've recovered a bit."

Sarah discovered that she was suddenly very hungry indeed and eventually, though he swore that he was not hungry, Peter managed to keep her company in good style. For some time eating took a distinctly greater priority than talking.

CHAPTER SIX

Life Underground

When the feasting had finished and Ederyn and the others were seated around the fire, Peter motioned to Sarah:

"Come on," he said.

"But I wanted to hear Aneryn sing."

"Never mind that now. I think we ought to go and look at Aunty."

Peter suddenly looked very serious and Sarah blushed. She had been tempted to selfishness yet again when others were in great need. She remained silent with embarrassment as she followed Peter swiftly down a corridor, the pillars of which were like young saplings filled with the most beautiful carvings of birds.

"Why," she thought to herself, "there must be just about every bird here that ever was, or ever will be. Oh, and I do like that little Puffin!"

She was wishing she could take a closer look when Peter made a sharp turn into the doorway of a room that she half recognised. It was the room where Peter had been brought out of his trance and one that was kept especially for nursing the sick. Peter having been moved to where Sarah had slept before.

In the glow of several small lamps, Peter and Sarah saw Aunt Myf laid on one of the beds. She was fast asleep and looked very peaceful. No one would suspect the trauma she must have suffered in this latest adventure.

"Except that her hair looks greyer," said Peter, looking keenly at her.

"They have calmed her."

Morvith was at their service once more. She stood behind them with a bowl of steaming water, which smelt sweetly of lavender and other herbs. Peter and Sarah stood aside to enable her to enter the room. Morvith crossed to Aunty's bed, washed her face and hands, plumped the pillows and brought blankets to cover her.

"It was the work of Orddu," said Morvith, "she thought that she was one of Bloddwedd's maidens. It is a very good thing Sarah, that you were able to bring her back to Arx Emain. She might have harmed herself without knowing what she was doing, poor thing."

"Why, what would she have done?" asked Sarah.

"Well, she would have done what all Bloddwedd's maidens did, of course."

"But what DID Bloddwedd's maidens do?" Peter asked, sharply.

Morvith gave Peter a very strange look, as if she expected him to know.

"They were all drowned in a lake!" she said, and tucked Aunt Myf firmly into the bed.

She then signed for the children to leave. They slipped silently out of the room, having given Aunty a kiss. Morvith began to bathe Aunt Myf's face again with the aromatic liquid.

"I do hope Aunt Myf will recover," said Sarah.

"Well," said Peter, as they retraced their steps to the Great Hall, "it happened to me and I'm OK now."

"Are you?" Sarah suddenly wondered, "Are you sure Peter?"

"I think I am. At any rate, my skin hasn't gone green and I haven't grown another head."

He laughed. Sarah laughed as they tried to make light of it. But thereafter, Sarah and Peter both wondered whether or not there was some permanent change in Peter.

As they re-entered the Great Hall they could hear Aneryn singing. She and Anir stood before Ederyn with the other Elves in a circle around them. It was a truly wonderful sight. A light seemed to glow around the pair. Was it from the many candles around the Hall or from the fire flickering in the hearth? Sarah could not tell, but thought it made Aneryn the most beautiful Lady that she had ever seen.

Anir took his turn with the song, which seemed to have many verses. Sarah took a firm hold of Peter's hand and led him into the Hall. They tiptoed to a place where they could sit just behind Ederyn and be in full view of the singers.

Anir had been singing in Elvish, but when the children came to sit down, either he had changed the language of his song to sing in English, or Peter and Sarah had gained the gift of understanding in a flash! Either way, this is some of the song they heard.

> The road was long, the night was old,
> The stars shone still, as jewels fair,
> To brave the dawn light pale and cold,
> In sky of pearl were shimmering.
> The wanderer lay sleeping there,
> 'Till ray of sun turn night to gold
> And wake him, light upon his hair,
> And on his raiment glimmering.
>
> He woke beneath the oak leaves green,
> To take the road he loves to roam.
> He walks by many men unseen,
> Alone through woods, untroubling;
> Until at last he reaches home
> 'Ere winter winds blow shrill and keen.
> O'er mountains tall and salt sea foam
> And rushing rivers, bubbling.
>
> With eager feet he wends his way
> Each spring, from care and sorrow free.
> He sings all summer through his lay,
> With field and forest listening.
> At last the salt wind o'er the lea
> That tells of water, dancing, gay;
> Blows him strong towards the sea
> Where sun on waves is glistening.
>
> And so through Autumn's misty haze,
> Sleepy forest, plain and hill,

The wanderer returns down ways
That long he has been following.
To home, beside a mountain rill,
That waits for him through summer days.
Of memories he has his fill,
And now shall rest, not sorrowing.

Anir finished singing. The Elves clapped and then, even
though by this time they were half asleep, Peter and Sarah heard
Aneryn begin to sing:

A lonely knight imprisoned
Was gazing far away,
He looked out towards the mountains
To where his freedom lay.

He saw the dew fall on the ground
And watched the fading light.
He longed to wander free once more
Away into the night.

But then he caught a fleeting glance,
A lady of perfect grace
Came wandering. The moon shone dim
Compared to the light in her face.

He fell at once in love with her
And called to the Lady fair;
At last she came towards the tower
And found the knight's cell there.

So every night she came to him,
Undying love he swore!

Then one day she brought the key
To unlock the tower door!

From the evil tower they soon were sped!
And passed from night to day;
To the knight's home atop the mountains,
And there they would ever stay.

The song ended and there was more applause. To Peter and Sarah it sounded like waves on the seashore, grating over the pebbles.

"Time for small folk to sleep, I think!"

Ederyn had turned around and noticed that they were almost in the land of dreams. He summoned Elves to escort them to their rooms, which were not far from the room where Aunt Myf lay. Soon they too were tucked up in bed and truly fast asleep.

It must have been towards dawn when Peter realised that he was in a dream. He dreamt that he was standing on a large rabbit warren in a wooded dell opposite Arx Emain. It was night.

Suddenly clouds above parted to reveal a full moon and stars. It was good to be outside and Peter thought that he should be feeling pleased. He did not. The air felt heavy, almost thundery, and the night ominous. All at once, Peter noticed something unusual. Around Arx Emain, almost making a full circle, were many huge standing stones. They were like all the stones that he knew could be seen every few hundred yards in this part of Wales.

"That's funny," he thought to himself," I don't remember seeing any stones here before."

He was just about to move away from the dell in order to investigate, when it seemed to Peter that the stones moved.

"It's as if they all took one step forward."

He breathed heavily. A few moments later, as he waited there, the same thing happened. He found that he could no longer move. Fear crept up on him and rooted him to the spot. Behind Arx Emain, a huge black shadow appeared; not like a cloud, a really thick black shadow.

Peter's tongue went dry and stuck to the roof of his mouth. He tried to cry out; to warn Ederyn, Anir and the Elves, but he could not. The stones moved again and the black shadow reached out above Arx Emain towards him. In his dream he fainted. When he opened his eyes again, he was still in bed and Sarah was shaking him awake.

"Peter wake up, wake up! You're having a bad dream, I know you are. Oh do wake up!"

"Hey, hey. I am awake and you are right. I've just had one heck of an evil dream. It seemed so awfully real, too."

"I had a dream as well," said Sarah, hugging Peter tight.

She sat on the edge of his bed while he woke himself up properly.

"What's the time?" asked Peter.

"I don't know, I took my watch off last night."

"Let's see. Hang on I've got mine somewhere!" he said, squinting in the light of the candle at his bedside, "Four thirty two precisely. Thank goodness for modern science."

He sat up.

"I'm quite awake now Sarah. What did you dream about?"

"It was weird. I felt as if I was flying over the countryside towards Foel Cwmcerwyn and I passed over a lake. As I went over, I saw Aunt Myf taking a swim in the lake. Then I woke up. Don't you think that was odd? What was your dream like? Can you say? You were screaming like anything."

"I'll say in a minute," said Peter, fumbling around for his clothes, "just as soon as I find Ederyn or Anir."

"But it was just a dream." complained Sarah.

"Was it?"

Peter looked at her, his face twisted into a grim smile so that she could not tell whether he was excited or terrified.

"Was it?" he asked her again, more urgently this time, "I think it's a warning! Go and find Morvith and see how Aunty is sleeping tonight."

Sarah turned to go but almost as if 'on cue', Morvith appeared at the door with a candle.

"Oh, you are both up already," she said, "Ederyn has sent for you."

"Is our Aunt all right?" asked Sarah.

"Yes. She sleeps, but she has been very restless all night. I believe something is happening outside. Ederyn has had messengers. They came through the North Tunnel at three o'clock and Ederyn and Anir have been with them until now."

"I'll just get dressed," said Sarah, and disappeared.

"Do you have any idea what news the messengers brought?" Peter asked.

"No," said Morvith, "Ederyn will tell you himself. He waits for you in the Hall of the Stone. You must meet him there."

At length Sarah arrived and Morvith said that she must go back to Aunt Myf.

"I have strict instructions that I am not to leave her alone. My friend Avaun sits with her at present, but I must go back."

She bowed to the children and walked away quickly down the corridor.

Peter and Sarah walked the opposite way to reach the Hall of the Stone. Peter strode down the corridor urgently with Sarah trotting behind him. When they came to the Hall of the Stone, the doors were open and light poured from the Hall.

Sarah seized Peter's arm as they came to the doors.

"The light is coming from the Stone!" she cried excitedly.

They passed through the massive doors and found Ederyn and Anir. Ederyn sat in the golden throne. Anir was standing at his right. Peter and Sarah came to the foot of the dais.

"Welcome, my little friends," said Ederyn, "I am glad you have arrived. We have a most serious decision to make."

He was staring hard at the children as he spoke, as if to know their thoughts, even before they had heard his news.

"Arddu has begun the attack," said Anir, simply, "and Gwyn is still over the sea."

"The scouts tell of the black shadow over Foel Drygarn and countless numbers of his creatures and those of Orddu massing upon the hills of the Prescelly range, and all around. Gwyn would want to move on them before their plans are complete, that I am sure of."

"The farmers hereabouts are much troubled," said Anir "the scouts have told me that it is almost as bad as the time that was before this time. They speak, not only of shadows, but also of a great black cat that prowls the hill, killing any animal that gets in its way. It terrifies any human that sees it. And there are other things too terrible to mention when the enemy is closing in on us."

Ederyn looked closely at Peter and Sarah.

"I see that you are troubled. What is the matter?" he asked.

"Oh, we have both had bad dreams," replied Sarah.

"And what did you dream?"

"I dreamt I was flying over the countryside towards the Prescellys and as I went over a lake, I saw Aunt Myf swimming in it."

"Well dreamt, little maid!" cried Ederyn, "It was a message, but one we were expecting. We have already doubled the guard on your Aunt. We do not wish her to fulfill the curse that Orddu has laid on her. She will not be safe until we have defeated all our enemies. What dream did you have, Peter?"

Peter described the dream that he had had as well as he could. When he had finished, Ederyn turned to Anir and whispered something. Anir left the Hall directly, stopping only to bow briefly to Sarah and Peter.

"Where did you send Anir?" asked Peter.

"He has gone to have the south eastern borders of our realm checked for enemy activity," said Ederyn.

Sarah was surprised that he answered Peter, whom she thought rather cheeky.

"Was my dream also a message?"

"Certainly," replied the Elf Lord, "but it must be checked to test out the truth of it. That is one of Arddu's greatest tricks. He will sow confusion in people's minds until they doubt whether things have happened, will happen or are happening in the present. It is better you put the whole thing away from your mind as it may be that this thing never happens. Arddu is the supreme liar. However, when we leave, we shall leave by another way."

"Leave!" cried both the children together, quite horrified by this suggestion.

"Yes, leave," said Ederyn, "Gwyn will need more than all the armies of Faerie put together. He will need the Samildanach, so he will have need of the Stone of Gardar to call them."

Peter thought he heard a musical sound come from the Stone when it was mentioned by Ederyn. It glowed ever brighter in its niche and seemed to begin a tuneful soft ring or hum.

"But I thought we were told never to leave here, not even in the gravest circumstance," said Peter.

"That is why I say that we have a most difficult decision to make and one where we do not have much time in which to make it."

Ederyn spoke softly, but there was an edge to his voice. Could even he be worried as to the outcome? Sarah wondered.

"My head tells me to ride at once to Gwyn and that you should remain here in safety. However, my heart tells me that you, Peter, in particular; are bound up with the fate of the Stone. I believe it is you who must carry it and perhaps even wield it in the battle that is to come. You are the one who may, in the end, decide the fate of Arx Emain and all who dwell within. We must meet with Gwyn before Arddu is ready to make a full attack. Now leave me for the present, little ones. I must consider all things and endevour to choose aright. Elves have a great disadvantage in that they are able to see 'round all the corners,' as they say! Now go both of you. Find yourselves some breakfast, and make it a hearty one. I do not know if or when you may have to leave."

Ederyn bowed his head in thought and Peter and Sarah tiptoed out of the room.

About an hour later, as Peter and Sarah were finishing off rather a large loaf of bread with mountains of butter and honey, Anir came flying through the door and marched purposefully towards them. He was dressed for travelling, booted and cloaked. A long sword showed under the folds of his cloak.

"Hmm, looks like this is it!" whispered Sarah.

"Haste, haste!" Anir called sharply, "You are to get ready right away and ride out with the maniple that will take the Stone of Gardar to Gwyn."

Peter gave Anir what they called within their family, 'an old fashioned look'.

"But I thought," he said.

Anir cut him short.

"Yes, yes! I know and I concur. This puts everything upon a knife-edge. I have spent the greater part of last night putting the opposing argument to Ederyn, but he will not be gainsaid."

Anir then 'hooshed' the children out of the Great Hall and down the corridor towards their rooms, scattering the Elves, who were approaching the Hall in order to take their breakfast, in all directions.

"You at least, Sarah, must stay here. You could help Morvith watch over your Aunt."

"Oh no, not this time!" said Sarah, "This time I am going with Peter. We shall stick together like glue!"

"Very well, but note this, my friends: I disagree entirely with your presence on this quest. You are only willing to go because you do not know what you will face."

"That's not quite true," said Peter "Sarah and I have both had a taste of the enemy. But anyway I think we have to try and finish Arddu off by whatever means are available to us. I found the Stone so I'd better be the one to look after it for Gwyn, if that is what I am meant to do."

"I agree with you, Bro," said Sarah emphatically, "we're both going and that is that!"

"Well, in the end I suppose it is up to you. It is your choice but if you do choose to ride with Ederyn you had better hurry up and pack. You may be away for several days, out there in the wild."

Anir bowed and left.

"Several days!"

Sarah's brain was suddenly jolted back to her real world, the world outside Arx Emain, where people do not deal daily with Elves. What was the date? How long was it to the end of the Summer Holidays, when Mother and Father were due to return from the Summer school to collect them from Aunt Myf's. With horror she realised that she did not know.

They both had very excellent digital watches that kept good time; even underground in the Elf Kingdom, but they did not have the date. Sarah had not thought until now, that it might be important. Summer Holidays always seemed to stretch on for ever. It was no good asking Peter, he must have lost count weeks ago -- WEEKS AGO!

Was it weeks or only days? Frantically she tried to cast her mind back to count the days, as she tried to find another set of warm clothes to put in the sack/bag that Morvith (probably) had provided. But it was no good.

At last she and Peter seemed to have collected all that was necessary and wandered out of their rooms with bags, enveloped in very large cloaks. Peter looked excited, Sarah looked worried. Inside the very large cloak, which bore a large patch in its lining, Sarah felt extremely harassed.

"I must tell Peter," she thought, "he must think about Mother and Father and the end of the holidays. Some fine holiday this turned out to be."

Sarah looked at Peter who was watching an increasing number of Elves passing down the corridor, bearing all sorts of gear for making war. Sarah prodded her brother, but he did not respond.

"I bet you're enjoying this," she said in a loud whisper, "this is real Action Hero stuff!"

"Eh, What?" replied Peter, whose interest was entirely taken up with the latest group of Elves.

These were carrying some very heavy boxes and Peter was very curious to see what was in them.

"Do you notice it, Sarah?"

"Notice what? Where's Anir gone? Didn't he say we'd got to hurry up and now he's disappeared? He's always disappearing, usually when we want him."

"Sarah look at the direction the Elves are taking with the baggage and boxes."

"Yes, yes, down to the Great Hall."

"Good girl!"

"What about it?"

"Don't you see?" said Peter in great excitement, "They are taking everything AWAY from the main gates."

111

"Well," said Sarah, thinking for a moment, "perhaps the Great Hall is a marshalling point."

"Oh, I don't think so," answered Peter, hopping from foot to foot, "I think they are going to the alternative exit. Come on, let's go and see."

"Shouldn't we wait for Anir?" Sarah hesitated.

"No, I bet he's gone to the back door to see how things are going. Don't you remember, it's as Ederyn said, 'We've got to leave by another way'."

"I don't see why you're so pleased," said Sarah, flatly determined to be unimpressed, "it's only a back door."

Peter was just going to flatten his sister with a singularly clever remark, when they saw Anir coming up the corridor towards them. He motioned to them to follow him and once again they found themselves in the Hall of the Stone. Anir knelt for a brief moment before the magical Stone in a way that was almost religious.

"As if he were in Church," Sarah put it afterwards.

Then he took a small bag from within his tunic, placed the Stone inside it and gave it to Peter.

"You are once again the Guardian of the Stone. Ederyn has decided it is right." he said, bowing deeply, "May you bear it to good fortune, may it bring you strength and power when you need it most and may the power of all powers bring you safely home."

With this benediction, Anir led them from the Hall and down a tunnel the children had not used before. Instead of going into the Great Hall, they passed down the left side of it. After a while Sarah noticed that they were going down a very gentle, but quite definite slope.

As they walked, Sarah pulled Peter by the sleeve.

"Do you know what day it is today? "

"No," replied Peter casually, "what day is it today?"

"I don't know," answered Sarah, miserably.

"Oh, I thought you were asking a rhetorical question," said Peter "don't you know, really?"

"No. And just think about this, while you're off on your great quest. What happens if Mother and Father arrive to collect us and we're still away? And how do we explain what's happened to Aunt Myf?"

Peter frowned. It was true; his thoughts had been too busy with the Stone to think of anything else. He could see that angry parents might pose a problem.

"Got a solution?" queried Sarah.

"No, but I'll think about it. Perhaps Anir knows the date. I'll ask him."

But before they could persue their thoughts, they were distracted entirely by one of the most wonderful things that they had ever seen.

The tunnel had been taking them downwards for some time but now it opened out into a huge cavern, even larger than the Great Hall, if that were possible. The walls were of carved stone, as was the case generally in the Elf Kingdom, but the upper parts were decorated with golden filigree of the most delicate kind.

Flowers, grasses, and insects, particularly butterflies, were described. A huge gold and crystal chandelier hung from the cavern roof and through the centre ran a sparkling underground stream, making a light ford over the pathway.

On the near side of the ford were gathered many horses and ponies. Elves were getting packs together and loading them onto the stouter of the animals. It appeared that here were gathered all the Elves Ederyn had brought from the north together with many of those from Arx Emain.

Before all stood Aneryn, with a great sword. She was dressed in a robe that shone silver, a silver coronet was in her hair and jewels of a deep blue were about her neck and round her wrists. A cloak swirled behind her, also of the deepest blue.

"This was my brother's sword, Anir. I give it to you. Bear it well."

Anir took the sword and exchanged it for his own. When it was buckled in place, he bowed to Aneryn once more. Suddenly, she took his hand.

"I hope it will not be long before we meet together once more, then you must promise not to leave us again."

"Lady, if I am fortunate enough to return here when all is done, then I shall be ready to make you that promise."

They gazed at each other silently for a moment, then embraced.

"I think they just got engaged," whispered Sarah in Peter's ear.

"Ssh!"

Peter gave her a brotherly dig in the ribs.

"Farewell, Anir," said Aneryn at last.

Then she turned to the children.

"Farewell Peter and Sarah. May you ever ride to good fortune."

Peter bowed as low as he could. It seemed to be the right thing to do. Elves then surrounded the children and Peter and Sarah were placed on two of the ponies. Anir was already astride his own horse. All were ready to leave. Then a thrill of excitement passed through all who were assembled.

"And there must be several hundreds of Elves here at least," thought Peter, but he did not have time to count them.

Ederyn appeared at last. He was magnificently arrayed with gold breastplate and shield. He leapt into the saddle and took his place at the head of the procession. Anir bent over towards Aneryn.

"This was my Mother's. Will you keep it for me?" he said, and passed a brooch to her, which she pinned immediately at the neck of her robe.

Ederyn raised his arm. It was the sign to depart. The legions of the Elves moved forwards. Aneryn remained at the centre of the cavern, waving. They crossed the ford. All minds, except possibly Sarah's, were on the way ahead.

A passage led them out of the cavern. They all passed out and again down into the dark depths. This passage was only very dimly lit, with small lamps placed onto wall recesses every few yards. They started out riding almost six abreast but as the passageway narrowed they could only ride two together.

This went on for a long time, until Peter and Sarah knew not if it were day or night. Only several hours later did the passage lead them upwards and outwards towards the real world, as Peter and Sarah liked to put it.

Finally the legions rode out into a wood in what must have been late afternoon. Ederyn halted them and bade them rest and eat. Peter and Sarah fell hungrily on some bread, cheese and fruit. Then they lay back on the grass and fell asleep.

"An engagement, definitely an engagement," murmured Sarah, as she drifted into unconsciousness.

CHAPTER SEVEN

A Sea Voyage

When Peter awoke, he saw stars above him. He stared at them for a while in silent joy. It was the first time that he had been outside Arx Emain for what seemed an age, though in all was probably only a few weeks, certainly less than a month. Somehow, time seemed to run differently in the underground kingdom.

"I'm free," he thought, "free at last!"

But then the Stone under his cloak dug him in the elbow.

"OK, OK, not quite free yet," he muttered.

"Awake at last, young master?"

It was Ederyn's voice. Peter turned and saw Ederyn and Anir both bending over him.

"You have slept well. Your sister sleeps yet!" said Anir, "Arise and eat with us, for we must move again soon."

"Are we safe?" said Peter, looking round as if he expected Arddu himself to appear from behind a tree.

"We are safe enough for the present," said Ederyn "we have come secretly, many miles away from Arx Emain and the Prescelly Mountains."

"When do we meet up with Gwyn?"

"Very soon. Come, wake your sister and come with us. There is to be a meeting to consider the next move."

Ederyn rose and left Anir to help Peter waken Sarah.

"Ugh!" she spluttered, as Peter shook her awake, "Why did I say I'd come?"

"Because you love your brother!" said Peter, "Come on Sis, this could be the last lap, and then perhaps we'll be free to go home."

"I'm coming. I must say though, just at this moment, an hours maths homework would be a welcome change from all this."

"I'd hardly put it that strongly," said Peter, "but I know what you mean."

"Come, Peter, Sarah, let us go and see what Ederyn is planning," said Anir, gently.

"Hey!" said Sarah, "Peter, have you asked Anir, you know -- what day it is?"

"You want to know the date?" broke in Anir, "Why it is Sunday, August the twenty ninth."

"Oh, my goodness!" Sarah jumped up, "Peter, when do we go back to school?"

"September thirteenth; keep your hair on! We've two whole weeks to get this mess sorted out."

"You make it sound like knitting," pouted Sarah.

Peter patted her arm.

"I only mean that we might just get time to help sort this adventure out and get out of it before school time, if we're lucky."

"I have every confidence that we shall succeed in our endevours!" joined in Anir, "This way!"

They passed through some very tall trees and came down into a hollow. Many Elves were standing round the hollow creating a ring, like a living fortress wall. They parted to let Anir and the children pass.

"I think I can hear the sea," said Sarah, surprised.

She pulled at Anir's cloak.

"Where are we? Are we near the sea?"

"We are quite near to St. David's," replied Anir, "we have come through one of the Elves' ancient escape routs. St. David's is a place that is sacred to you and to those who follow older ways. It is a holy place and so we are safe here for a little while. Elves have often come here in times of trouble. It is from near here that they can sail to their kinsfolk over the seas, to Ireland and beyond."

The three stepped slowly down a narrow path into the hollow. In the centre of the dip was a fire. In the firelight Peter and Sarah could see Ederyn seated at the far side of the ring.

Anir passed by the fire and went to sit beside him. He signed to Peter and Sarah to sit at his feet. Most of the Elves who had been standing guard around the hollow now came within the fire's light and sat down in perfect silence. It struck Peter that they were commanded to do so.

"Of course," he thought, "they can communicate by thought alone."

Ederyn raised both his arms:

"Tomorrow, fellow friends and loyal subjects of Gwyn-ap-Nudd; tomorrow we shall rejoin our King and the armies from the Isles Overseas. Welcome, again, to our friends from the

North Kingdom, and our deepest thanks. Dear friends, tomorrow marks the beginning of what we all hope to be a final defeat for Arddu, The Evil One, and the end of all his kind."

A low roar of approval came from the gathering, and the occasional clank of sword on shield could be heard. Ederyn raised his arms once more to speak, but before he could continue his speech, an Elf came into the ring; half running, half staggering, down the path towards them. He managed to bow to Ederyn, then went down on one knee.

"Lord Ederyn, your brother the Lord Gwyn-ap-Nudd has sent me."

"What news, brother Elf?"

"Many farmers are gathering before the Crymych arms. Gwyn thinks that many hundreds of the country folk will gather there. They are angry at the Great Beast because it is killing their animals, and they have determined upon hunting it down. They are armed."

"Very good, very good indeed!" Ederyn smiled, "And what would my King, what is his command?"

"That you make all haste to the meeting place that was agreed."

"Very well, then, and where do Gwyn and his armies lie now, exactly?"

"Not far from Ceredigiawn, My Lord."

"Good, good!"

Ederyn turned to face the assembled legions and cried out:

"We ride, we ride! To arms Elven Folk!"

All assembled rose and dashed spear or sword on shield, or raised their bows and arrows towards the stars, for there were many skilled in archery there.

"But!" Ederyn cried out again, even louder than before so that everyone was immediately hushed, "First we are forced to take ship and sail."

Peter and Sarah looked about them. No one seemed particularly surprised. Anir sat with his head in his hands, looking resigned.

"First Maniple, I command you to depart and make ready the ships," Ederyn said, and immediately, about a hundred Elves left by the narrow path as silently as the wind passes through the short grasses on the hilltops.

Sarah tugged at Anir's cloak:

"Why are we sailing?" she asked.

"Why did we come out here through the secret tunnel?" asked Anir, half to himself, "Arddu, who by the way is the Great Beast the Messenger spoke of, has blocked the front entrance to Arx Emain. Just as you saw in your dream, Peter, there are what appear to be giant stones moving ever closer to Gwyn-ap-Nudd's front door! They are Arddu's creatures -- shape-shifters."

Peter was suddenly very glad that they had not had to brave going out that way.

"Arddu supposes that all the Elves are blocked up inside Arx Emain. He does not know about the tunnel."

"Why is that?" asked Peter.

"Because the last time that the Elves were in conflict with the Evil One, they did not have the tunnel and had to fight their way out. That time Arddu had a friend who turned himself into a great boar with tusks like battering rams and bristles as sharp as razors. Gwyn-ap-Nudd had been assisting King Arthur in the hunting of him. They went from Porth Cleis to the Severn River; and great tribulation there was in the chase. This time they are ready for Arddu."

As Anir spoke, Ederyn was giving orders for a speedy departure. The Elves were leaving the clearing in companies of about a hundred each.

When the Twenty-fifth Maniple was announced, Anir told Peter and Sarah to follow him. Ederyn sprang to his horse and

led the way to the beach. Anir, Peter and Sarah were to the rear
and with them, also rode the messenger of Gwyn-ap-Nudd,
whose name was Eri.

They found themselves on the beach. Great rafts were being
paddled to and fro with Elves, horses and supplies. They were
making for great grey ships that were moored some way distant
from the shore. To the East Peter noticed that the sky lightened
slightly. Dawn must be approaching.

"Goodness!" said Sarah, "Everything looks very well
organised."

"And so it is," said Anir, "they have had all this planned for
many hundreds of years. Gwyn may have been caught out once,
but he will never be trapped again."

"Shall he win this time too?" said Peter, giving voice to the
fears that he and Sarah had spoken of only in secret.

"Why, of course. Do not fear!" Anir answered gently, "Do we
not possess the Stone of Gardar?"

Peter had forgotten about it momentarily, in all the
excitement. He patted the bag that contained it and wished that
he could look at it again. Before he was able to bring it out,
however, they were pushed and pulled onto a raft, from where at
length they came to a great sailing ship with a ramp up to the
hold.

Up the ramp went Elves, horses, Anir Peter and Sarah until all
were aboard the ship. This was the last ship to sail. From the
deck, Peter and Sarah watched the land slip away and wondered
what might happen next.

The sun reddened the sky in the East, out to sea. The land lay
grey in the chilly dawn and a light breeze filled the huge sail of
the Elven ship. Everything seemed to be grey. At the prow they
came upon Ederyn and Anir, who were deep in thought, or
conversation.

Elves have the gift of conversing by thought alone, and the children wondered if Anir had learnt the knack of it by being with them so much. Their guesses seemed to be confirmed as Anir turned towards them as they passed.

"We have just decided that we shall take today as a rest day. Be sure to take your ease on board this ship, while you can. We shall keep out to sea in the mist. Few will notice us sailing up the coast, not even the Fishguard Ferry to Ireland will see us! Tonight at the latest we shall all be moored off Ceredigiawn Island, and tomorrow..."

"Tomorrow, we join Gwyn-ap-Nudd and defeat Arddu!" joined Ederyn, "And," he looked at Peter suddenly, "it is round about twenty of your miles to our mooring point. If the breeze could waken a little, we should be there the sooner. In the meantime, breakfast is waiting."

He waved his hand towards the after deck where a cold buffet was being laid out. Peter hurried over to get their share. The travelling and the early hour made them ravenously hungry.

"He knew what I was thinking," said Peter, chewing on a meat filled roll.

"Well, he's almost an Elf himself, I suppose. More like them than us. A ' betwixt and between'," said Sarah, adding, "I don't like this calm, though, it's the lull before the storm. If only..." she began, and Peter joined in.

"Mother and Father had not gone to the Summer School all summer."

Sarah giggled, "You're doing it now, Peter. You thought my thought!"

"Pure coincidence, and anyway, we're very close. Families often do that."

"Yes, I suppose so. Well, at least Ant Myf is safely tucked up in bed."

"Oh, I do hope so!" said Peter, rather more vehemently than usual, "I really, really do!"

Anir was right about the invisibility of the Elvish fleet. The Fishguard Ferries plied their trade regularly all that day and never saw them. Though to be fair, there was a great deal of heat haze, as the weather was beginning to turn thundery, as it often does at the end of a long hot summer.

The sea was calm and the winds were not helpful. The ships had to ' tack' up the coast before they came anywhere near Fishguard, and crossing Newport Bay the wind dropped to a whisper so that they almost had to row. It was twilight when the ships began to moor off Cardigan Island. The air was by this time, hot, still and very heavy.

"I'm sure it's going to thunder soon," said Sarah anxiously.

Peter leant over the bow.

"I wonder if we will be close to the fighting?" he said to himself, in a very depressed tone of voice.

The feeling of foreboding that had sat in the pit of his stomach all day was growing stronger every minute. The heaviness of the weather and the proximity of electrical storms made the feeling much worse. The sun set in a sickly hue, colouring the western sea with the pinks and greens, yellows and greys of imminent bad weather. In the distance the odd rumble of thunder could be heard.

Peter and Sarah could not imagine what a battle might be like, never mind one that might coincide with a thunderstorm. They all spent a most restless night. Peter paced up and down the deck with the Stone in his hand.

When Anir or Ederyn were not around, nor any of the Elves he took it out of its bag and ran his fingers over its strange surface. Whether it was the approaching storms, or whether it was that they were drawing nearer to Arddu, he did not know, but as the night wore on he was sure that he felt the Stone vibrate. In the darkness he could also see its faint glow growing stronger.

Sarah watched him until she could bear it no longer and in the early hours dragged him down into the hold, where there were soft mattresses laid down for them, and told him firmly to go to sleep.

"I know it's all awful," she said, "I'm feeling just as hot and sticky as you are, but I'm going to sleep if I can, and you've got to try too."

Peter lay down and Sarah threw herself down next to him and slept a deep dreamless sleep. Peter tossed and turned until he finally managed to sleep a little. It was a deep sleep, to begin with, but later he did dream. It was like a Cartoon Film.

He saw a beautiful maiden coming towards him. She was either covered with, or dressed in the most beautiful flowers. Every flower that he had ever seen, from the dog rose to the most exotic lilies, seemed to be part of her costume. She came nearer and nearer to him, saying nothing, her feet passing over what looked like water. Was it the sea or a lake? That she was walking on water did not appear at all remarkable, but then, it was a dream.

Nearer and nearer she came, and just as Peter saw her face move, as if she were going to speak, the face changed into that of Aunt Myf, a sad, pale face, streaked with some kind of slime.

"I am Bloddwedd's...." said the vision, and then promptly faded into darkness.

"Oh, my goodness!" Peter sat up panting,

"What is it? What is it?"

He had woken Sarah.

"I don't think Aunt Myf is safe any more. I had a dream, I saw it all."

"Well, there's nothing we can do about it from here, so just calm down, will you. You've got to do your Super Hero, Action Chap thing today, or whatever."

"Oh DO shut up, Sarah!" said Peter, irritably, "I want to think."

"Humph!" said Sarah, "Get you!" and she swept off to find something to eat with all the indignation that she could muster!

The storm had not broken as yet and you could cut the atmosphere with a knife.

The Elves were gathered on the upper deck. Most of them had eaten and those who had were making ready to disembark. Ederyn had given out his orders and no one seemed to be taking any notice of the children.

Sarah grabbed what was left of the food and filled every spare nook and cranny of their luggage with bread and fruit. Then she took a decent portion for herself and Peter as breakfast. When she returned below decks, Peter was still sitting gloomily, all of a heap.

Sarah almost threw his breakfast at him. Like an automaton, Peter picked it up and ate. Sarah watched him. Feeling a little more sympathetic by degrees, she patted his shoulder.

"Don't worry," she said, "I don't expect they'll let us anywhere near the fighting.

"THEY won't!" said a voice behind them.

Anir had come to look for them to bid them get ready for going ashore. Sarah let out a large sigh of relief.

"You won't come near the thick of it, not if I can help it," said Anir.

Peter brightened visibly. He jumped up and, slinging his bag over his shoulder, followed Anir to the upper deck. Trotting behind them came Sarah, and soon they were going down the ramp to yet another raft, where Ederyn and some other Elves were waiting.

"Be quick. We must be at the place of the White Church by midday if possible," Ederyn grumbled.

He turned to Peter and Sarah and spoke low:

"You must stay by me as much as you can until we meet Gwyn again. Then, during the punishment and retribution that is to be meted out to Arddu, Orddu and all their minions, you must stay by Gwyn. You must not move from his side, or all may be lost. Anir has his special orders and will guard you all he can. If the worst should come to the worst, I have brought a short sword for you Peter and a dagger for you, Sarah."

"But Anir said we should not get near the fighting," said Sarah, perplexed.

"I said: if the worst should come to the worst. Use them only in greatest need," repeated Ederyn.

Then he turned away to speak again with Anir.

Sarah looked at the dagger with disgust.

"I suppose one might use it as a large paper knife or as a kebab at a barbecue," she muttered, "I hope they don't really expect me to use this."

Peter felt awed as he looked at the short sword. It was magnificently worked and had some kind of inscription in gold on the blade. The hilt shone with gold and precious jewels.

"Fit for a prince!" he thought.

The raft began to jump up and down in the surf at the beach. Everyone got off the raft and walked to the sands in the shallow waves. They passed silently up the beach. Although Peter and Sarah had just eaten their breakfast, it was in fact midday and should have been luncheon.

Amazingly, the passage of the Elves up the beach was seen, or it should be said noticed, by nobody. Most tourists were at their own lunch and the arrival of the last army out of Arx Emain coincided with a heavy thundershower.

Only one elderly lady wondered why there were so many horses on the sands today, as she looked out between the raindrops from the window of her B&B. But then, she was on the look out for strange happenings.

Ederyn gathered his troops together. Orders were passed down the lines and they set off on the final journey to meet Gwyn-ap-Nudd and the Kindred from Overseas. It rained. Thunder rain like descending stair rods accompanied the army all that afternoon.

They skirted round Cardigan, or Ceredigiawn as the Elves called it, vaguely following the river until they were almost at Cilgerran Castle. Then Ederyn doubled back to head towards Eglwyswrw and then down to Eglwyswen, the place of the White Church. By teatime, so his stomach told him, Peter guessed that they were near Llanfair-Nant-Gwyn, and getting ready to cross the river Nevern.

"Cheer up," said Anir, "nearly there now."

And he grinned as the rain dripped off his hood, down his nose and fell 'plop' onto his saddle. Peter and Sarah were no more comfortable. Sarah's cloak had begun to stick to her arms and as she looked at Peter she could see the water streaming down his face. She hardly noticed crossing the river as none of them could have been wetter than they were already.

Outside Eglwyswen, a sympathetic landowner had placed fields at Gwyn's disposal. There were several tents up and more to be put up. The fields were surrounded by little copses and hedges and spinneys; so that from a distance not much could be seen.

Ederyn led the bedraggled army into the encampment. At once they were all made welcome. Tents seemed to be springing up everywhere, now. Horses were led away and as if by magic, Elves were everywhere, helping each other to food and dry clothing within each canvas castle. Above them, mists lay heavy, drowning the view of the Prescelly Mountains and the heights of Foel Drygarn.

Ederyn was shortly drawn into his brother's tent and Anir followed with Peter and Sarah at his heels. There was great rejoicing at the meeting of Gwyn-ap-Nudd and Ederyn. After embracing each other heartily, Gwyn turned to the others.

"Well done; well done indeed! All is now ready for the morrow."

Anir, Peter and Sarah bowed. Gwyn beckoned Peter forwards.

"Have you kept the Stone?"

"Yes, Lord!" said Peter, and drew it out of its bag and gave it to Gwyn, who looked at it closely and then gave it back.

"No! No!" he said, "You shall keep it until it is the time for using it, and then only if it is absolutely necessary. Then either I myself or even you, Peter will know what should be done with it."

Peter took a pace backwards.

"You will not leave my side now, not you or your sister and Anir is to guard you as much as he can," Gwyn said sternly.

Peter thought that Anir looked put out. As if he, a bold fighting man, had been asked to play at being a nanny. Gwyn ignored him and spoke to Ederyn.

"We hope to start before dawn. We shall go the back way and fall on them from Foel Cwmcerwyn, while the farmers will come upon them from Mynachlogddu. They have the easier road and a shorter march from Crymych.

"As far as we know a good proportion of the enemy is still at Arx Emain, guarding your front door," said Ederyn.

"Good, splendid!" Gwyn smiled, a most merry smile, "I do hope Arddu is with them."

"He may well be. We hope he still thinks that I am trapped within. Aneryn and those who are left will be encouraging that idea," said Ederyn.

"Look to the maid!" said Anir sharply.

With horror, Peter, who had been caught up in the excitement of the discussion over battle plans, had not noticed Sarah getting greener and greener.

Since they had come into the tent, the humidity of the weather, the heaviness of the wet clothing and her empty stomach had all combined to make her feel most peculiar. Anir and Ederyn just managed to catch her as she fell down in a faint.

They laid her on Gwyn's very own bed, which was behind a screen and left Peter to care for her. In fact she was not out cold for long and felt a complete idiot when she came round. Anir returned a few minutes later.

"I shall not sleep tonight, nor will most of the Elves, but you must," he said.

He pulled out some sheepskins and made a bed for Peter.

"Sleep now, and wake strong for what may come at dawn, or before."

And so they slept, but not until both had had a good go at the provisions they had packed away and also put on dry clothes.

Early next morning they were woken by Eldol and Echel, who brought them water for washing and drinking, and some dry cloaks. It was still dark, so it must have been very early morning.

They made a quick breakfast and were packing up when Gwyn himself appeared. Peter bowed low and Sarah got up from the floor. Gwyn made them stop.

"You are to remain by my side from this moment on, until either Arddu or the Elf Kingdoms are finished. We shall be friends and friends do not have to bow to each other every time they meet. Come! It is time to go and seek out what fate decrees should come to pass."

Peter had thought that if they were to fall upon Arddu from the dizzy heights of Prescelly Top, that he and Sarah would find themselves doing an imitation of the S.A.S. up the hillside that morning.

In fact, he gathered from Gwyn that the Vanguard of the army, which by now numbered thousands, had done precisely that somewhat earlier. When their horses were brought to them by Eldol, they were told that they would be riding to Foel Cwmcerwyn via Crosswell, on the Nevern road. They were going with the rear guard for Ederyn had also gone ahead with about half those on horseback.

"We shall ride very calmly and quietly to join the rest of the armies," said Gwyn.

"Where is Anir?" asked Sarah as they trotted out of the camp.

"He has gone to lead the farmers from Crymych to Mynachlogddu so that we shall all converge on Arddu at the same time. He will think it is only the farmers come to rattle their pitchforks at him. But when we sweep down from the hills, he will find out differently."

"What about the stones round Arx Emain?" asked Peter.

"Messengers reported last night that they had gone. I have sent Echel with a small party to find out where they have gone. You are correct, Peter. It would not do to have them come upon us from behind. Although there were not too many of them, for the main part of Arddu's mighty army is under the Prescelly Mountains. It might prove an embarrassment yet."

Peter wriggled in his saddle. It was slightly uncomfortable to be in the company of those who could read his thoughts.

Sarah was still anxious.

"What about Anir, though? Ederyn said he was going to guard us."

"And so he is, so he is, when the battle proper begins he will return to defend you. He has gone for a little while only. When the farmers are in place he will return. You see not many humans can or will see us. They can only see Arddu and his creatures if he wills it. Also, they can only see us if I will it. Many who do not believe in other worlds will see nothing at all, save the Great

Beast of the Prescellys! And as many of his ugly creatures as he chooses to reveal to them. That will depend on how he sees the danger to himself, or how weak he becomes."

By now they were passing through Crosswell, leaving the Nevern River to their right. Dawn was beginning to glimmer faintly in the East. Thank goodness it had stopped raining sometime in the night, but now felt extremely hot and humid.

"More rain on the way," thought Peter.

The dawn light grew and in the early morning sunshine nature's diamonds glittered everywhere. Gwyn spurred his horse on, and the others followed him. Fearless, he led them at a very brisk trot along the mettled road.

"Onwards and up!" cried the legions of Elves behind them.

"Onwards and up!" cried the rest.

A blue flag with a Gold Hill surrounded by trees was unfurled. They were almost at Foel Cwmcerwyn now. When they finally came to the cairn, Peter gasped: an army of thousands was standing at the ready armed with spears, bows and swords; flags and banners blowing in the dawn wind.

The sky was clear and it seemed to Sarah that they were only waiting for a sign to start. She and Peter kept right behind Gwyn as they were bid. Peter clutched the Stone to his breast and drew his sword, which gleamed and glittered in the sun.

Sarah was so nervous that she began to have hiccups. She wished heartily that she were a hundred miles away from there.

CHAPTER EIGHT

The Battle!

It seemed that the Elvish armies waited for an age for anything to happen. There sat Gwyn on his magnificent white stallion, his armour and weaponry shining in the sun, with all present resting their eyes on him waiting for the signal to move. Only Sarah's occasional 'hic' broke the silence around them.

It was not until well after seven that they noticed mists rising from the old Blue Stone quarry at the foot of the Prescellys. Far away a vague clamour could be heard, as if the huntsmen were out. Horns were blowing, metal clashed on metal and voices were raised in anger -- shouting; but what were they shouting? Peter and Sarah could not hear.

It was the farming community marching down to Mynachlogddu. The mists issuing from the quarry began to thicken and rise upwards. Peter shivered;

"This is no ordinary mist," he whispered, "this is from the enemy."

Gwyn looked down at him.

"You are right Peter. Arddu is making ready to attack. Soon I shall signal our reply."

He raised his sword above his head where it shone so all could see it. The voices and general commotion from the angry farmers grew louder, the mist in the valley thickened.

A faint sound as of a trumpet blast came from deep in the ground beneath their feet. Gwyn brought his sword down sharply until it pointed to the ground. Straightway about half those on foot went down the sides of the mountain in order to draw whatever was under Mount Prescelly out from it, and to make sure they were caught between Elves and farmers.

For a while this plan worked very well. Arddu was not ready to reveal himself at the start and most of his creatures, which issued forth from the mountain, were easily dispatched by Elven archers.

Peter and Sarah felt superfluous. The battle was going very well and looked to be soon over. There had been no need for them to attend after all. A hand touched Sarah's arm. It was Anir at last! Peter and Sarah smiled with relief as he strode over to Gwyn to report on the battle below them. They could not quite hear what was said but things seemed to be going well.

Gwyn-ap-Nudd was nodding and smiling. An Elf brought a horse for Anir and he took up his position in front of Peter and Sarah. So that they could no longer quite see what was going on. After another hour or so more Elves left the hill to assist those below. Screams and yells of the most bloodcurdling kind could be heard.

The mists coming from the front gate of Arddu's kingdom grew thicker. Because all were looking down to see how the battle below was going, all but the scouts forgot to look up. A huge cloud, like a thundercloud, was growing over their heads.

Eldol suddenly appeared on the Roman road that comes from Foel Drygarn. He ran as fast as he was able for the many obstacles on the way. A first rumble of thunder was heard. Peter was watching the Elf King whose face became suddenly stern and grim.

"The Twenty-fifth Maniple must take up their positions," he ordered, and almost immediately, Eldol went off with them towards Bedd Arthur and Foel Drygarn.

"Why?" thought Peter, "Why are they going away from the battle that is raging below us to some old pile of stones?"

But this time neither Gwyn nor Anir answered as the first drops of rain from the impending storm began to fall.

If Peter and Sarah had thought that they were in for 'just a storm' they were badly mistaken. The whole of the sky to the southeast appeared to have turned completely black. Peter noticed that rain already fell on the villages eastwards of the Prescelly range.

Because the sun was still shining over Newport and Cardigan, this made the skies look even blacker, or was that the entire truth of it? The valleys below were also pitch black with a mist or cloud or other kind of noxious steam issuing forth from the gloomy portals of Annwm, the very gates of that which some have called 'the nether regions' or 'Hell'.

"Arddu is about to reveal himself and his plan. Stand firm Peter and Sarah. Guard them well, Anir! And Peter, do not seek the power of the Stone too early, until I or Anir tell you."

"Why should Gwyn need the Stone? Aren't Arddu's creatures having the worst of it down there in the Quarry?" asked Peter.

Gwyn was looking round about him, preoccupied with his own plans. Anir provided the reply.

"The creatures that poured from the Front Gate have been worsted, but that is only the beginning. The farming people are now searching for the Beast in earnest; but there is more than one doorway into Annwm. Another gate is at 'Bedd Arthur'. Somewhere in history, I suspect, the name was changed from 'Bedd Arddu' and the two were confused. Gwyn has a good idea of what the Dark One may do. He may try to drive us into the Quarry. He can try, but as long as we hold the Stone, he cannot succeed. Look out , here comes the storm."

Anir was right. The black clouds had filled all the sky. Thunder cracked, lightning crackled and the rain came down in torrents; filling cracks and gullies and flowing like rivulets down the mountainsides. All anyone could do was huddle in the saddle and brace themselves against the storm.

It felt as if it went on for ever. Sarah thought she would rather be under her horse than on it, and Peter wondered when the next move would be made.

As the thunder passed overhead and clouds began moving over Cardigan, Peter noticed dark shapes to the south of them. They looked like a forest, but they were moving!

"Now we know what happened to the shape shifters, Anir," said Gwyn.

Peter and Sarah noticed the forest move again.

"I never did think there were quite so many trees over there when we walked over these tops at the beginning of our holiday," muttered Peter, "there's the forest to the west, but there wasn't one down there."

"Can you see what sort of trees they are?" said Sarah.

"No!" said Peter, squinting in the rain, "It's too dark and they are not near enough to us yet."

A huge crack of thunder peeled overhead at the same time as lightning lit up the hill tops to the north. They saw a black shadow moving atop one of the cairns.

"Arddu shows himself at last!" said Gwyn.

"The Beast of Annwm comes!" cried Anir with a great shout.

He was answered from below:

"The Beast! The Beast comes!"

The farmers, not having found the beast at the Quarry, had begun the ascent of Prescelly Top.

"The Beast!" roared back Anir and Peter and Sarah and the army of the Elves.

Gwyn was smiling again, a secret smile. Then he laughed at the height of the storm and Sarah heard him singing.

> Lord of the Thunder!
> Lord of the rain,
> Oak trees come marching
> To hills from the plain.
>
> Sure footed is my horse
> On the day of battle.
> I have seen your plan
> And shall not flinch in the saddle.
>
> Oak may be felled
> Or crushed under stone.
> Arddu; this days end
> Shall witness your ruin!

Crack! Lightening flashed overhead once more, illuminating the whole mountain range. The great Beast was moving towards them from the direction of the cairns. He was at the head of a huge army of every kind of strange creature: witches and their familiars, half human looking monsters, wolves, pigs or boars and many other weird animals. Orddu was not far behind.

Peter could feel their presence before he could see them. Twisting round in the saddle, he saw the trees travelling swiftly towards them. Soon they would cross the road and be on their way up to Prescelly Top. He shuddered.

"Forward!"

Gwyn signalled the attack. Peter and Sarah did not know whether to follow or not. Anir decided for them by taking hold of their reins.

"The trees are coming to push us off the top and down to the old Quarry, or so the Dark One plans. Gwyn's attack, he supposes, will be beaten off by the army coming from his northern gate. However, we shall have assistance from Ederyn and the others, and the farmers are still on their Beast hunt. We are going to follow Gwyn, But...!" he looked round taking note of the situation.

"Get down off your horses!" he commanded them, "We are going roundabouts! Follow me!"

They left the horses, who immediately ran off behind the attacking Elves. Anir led them down the other side of the hills, not too far from the tops but far enough away from the action that they could not be seen. He made them walk at first, but as they got nearer the centre of the battling armies, he made them crouch down and crawl among the heather, bracken and bilberry bushes.

"Take this ring!" said Anir to Sarah, pressing something into her hand, "If you keep the stone inside your hand, it will make you invisible. Have you the Stone of Gardar, Peter?"

"Yes!"

"Do you know what to do?"

"I think so."

"Come then, this is the last gasp."

As they walked towards the battlefield, the noise was terrific! Thunder and lightening played and through the storm the two opposing armies were now drawn to hand to hand fighting. It was not a nice thing to see.

The Beast, Orddu who had assumed the form of a she wolf, and all their creatures, had had the best of several hundred of Gwyn's troops. Any of the farmers who were close to the Old Ways had joined in. The others worried the Beast but could never get near to him. Some had brought shotguns but of course, as it was not a flesh and blood animal, bullets just went straight through.

Sarah turned the stone of the ring into her hand and vanished. She felt too afraid to follow Anir any further, and chose a large rock to hide behind. She closed her eyes and hoped that Peter really did know what to do with the Stone!

The fighting was desperate. Anir hacked a way through to Gwyn who was making a stand on a small cairn opposite Arddu who was getting nearer and nearer. Orddu was at his side, laughing and howling in joy at the Elves discomfiture.

Peter followed Anir as best he could, turning the Stone over and over. The trees had come up behind Gwyn's troops, just as everyone had feared, forcing a confrontation. There was no escaping the Dark One.

Finally, Arddu came face to face with Gwyn. He had transformed his shape in part to be half a man. They did not speak, they just looked at each other for an interminable time. The whole battlefield became silent. This was a battle of wills. Gwyn raised his sword, Arddu replied with his, and they were at once locked in mortal combat.

Peter looked round. Anir was leaning on his sword, breathing hard. The trees were strung out on the hilltops driving a good part of Gwyn's army and the farmers right into the path of Arddu's creatures. The situation seemed irretrievable. Many of the Elves were dead or very badly wounded.

Eldol would never return to Arx Emain and Ederyn appeared to have been mauled by the Beast, he was covered in blood. It is not pleasant to see friends suffer in such a way. The Stone glowed in Peter's hands. The Ogham letters burned his brain until he instinctively knew what they wanted him to say:

"It is time!" he thought and trembled, "I can read the words, I know what they say."

And as he stood beside Anir, without waiting for any word of command from Anir or from Gwyn, he began to read aloud in a trembling voice.

"Oak that grows on battle mound,
Where crimson torrents drench the ground
Bring woe to him in darkness drowned.

Oak that grows through years of woes
Mid battle's broils unequalled throes,
A dreadful death his reign will close."

Peter's voice rose louder and louder. Arddu and Gwyn ceased their fight. All stood as if transfixed.

"Oak that grows on hill and plain
Where gushes blood of warriors slain,
See! The Samildanach come again!"

Peter's voice rose to a shriek. Sarah peeped through invisible fingers.

The glowing Stone dropped through Peter's hands as it became heavier and heavier. As in a trance he saw the Stone grow, form and transform itself. Larger and larger it grew until the aperture in the top of the Stone formed itself into a gateway once again, but this time it was huge! Beings appeared from within; similar in form to the Elves, but translucent and shining with golden light. In all there were about nine of them.

"Who calls on the power of the Samildanach?"

"I suppose I did," said Peter, shaking all over with fright.

"Who asks the power of the Samildanach?"

"Gwyn-ap-Nudd, King of the Elves, Lord of Arx Emain!" shouted Gwyn, taking charge.

"What is your bidding," sang the Golden Beings.

"The destruction of the Evil One, Arddu!" said Gwyn, "And all his armies."

"It shall be as you will," replied the beings.

However, before they began, Anir who had woken from the trance like state which had befallen them all, took up his sword and thrust it into the chest of Arddu. The shadowy figure staggered as the leader of the Samildanach stepped through the Stone portal just in time to finish him off.

"Ugh!" thought Peter, as something like black blood seeped from the wounds. The body of Arddu half man, half Black Beast turned into a dark fog and was gathered into the blackness of the storm clouds, which were passing overhead, and he was never seen again in those regions.

Gwyn-ap-Nudd, the Elves and the golden Samildanach then fell on the rest of Arddu's army with extreme fury. Orddu was slain by Gwyn himself. The golden people had the power to turn many of Arddu and Orddu's creatures into what they really were: pigs, dogs and cats and the like. Then the farmers and the Elves were easily able to dispatch them. The trees were also returned to their own shapes and sent packing.

At the end of the afternoon not many 'creatures' were left on the Prescelly Tops. Those who were able to escape made for the

North gate or the Quarry gate, but very few were fortunate enough to do so.

Peter felt extremely pleased as he had personally killed several half goblin/half pig things and something that was the size of a large hound, but looked like a werewolf. Anir was by his side, leaning on his sword, but this time there was a cut on his shoulder from which blood oozed slowly.

Gwyn had returned to the stone portal with the leader of the Samildanach. They exchanged looks then conversed in a strange language.

"I expect he's saying 'Thank you'," thought Peter to himself, "but it seems to take a long time."

A hand squeezed his. It was Sarah, who had decided that it was safe to stop being invisible.

"It's all turned out all right, then," she said.

"Seems so," said Peter.

And together they watched Gwyn and the chief of the Samildanach as they stood by the stone portal. The rest of the Golden Beings were already starting their return journey through the gate to wherever it was they came from.

Gwyn turned sharply to look at Peter and Sarah.

"Come!" he said, "You have earned a reward. Is there anything you wish for?"

"Oh yes!" said Peter, and without thinking at all, "I wish that Father and Mother were here."

"And I wish that Aunt Myf could be quite safe," said Sarah.

"Your wishes are granted. May the power of all powers ever be with you," said the leader of the Samildanach.

Then he bowed to Gwyn.

"Keep the Gardar Stone safe. Farewell, Lord of the Elves," he said.

"Farewell," said Gwyn and returned the bow.

The leader went back through the portal but before the gateway disappeared, through it from the other side came---

"Mother!" said Peter.

"Father!" said Sarah.

Their parents stood on the hilltop completely 'gobsmacked,' as Father said later. Peter and Sarah just took each of them by the hand and held tightly on to them while the Stone portal closed and Gwyn went to pick it up. He then gave it to Peter.

"Let your parents touch the Stone, it will help explanations later on."

Peter gave it to Father who passed it to Mother who passed it back to Gwyn. He bowed low to all then placed the Stone inside his jerkin, under his tunic. Then he turned to Anir.

"You are to escort these people to their rightful dwelling and then meet us at Arx Emain as soon as you are able. I am sure your return will be swift."

Gwyn leapt on to his horse, which Echel had brought to him. Ederyn and the other wounded were being borne away on stretchers and on horseback. The army of the Elves prepared to leave for Arx Emain. Once again, as the storm clouds cleared away, sun glinted on armour and weapons, though now they were all battle stained.

The farmers left for home also, satisfied that the Beast had gone and a few had got wild boar carcasses out of it.

"Nothing like a nice piece of roast pork!" they said as they went off to celebrate their victory at the Crymych Arms.

Anir stood with Peter and Sarah and Mother and Father watching Gwyn and the army pass Prescelly Top and make for the Nevern to Haverfordwest road. They would march by the side of it, too exhausted not to risk the occasional sighting, until able to take to open land and the hidden paths that lead to Arx Emain.

Someone coughed behind them, which made everyone, except Anir, jump nearly ten feet in the air. But it was only Eri, Gwyn's messenger, with their horses and two more for Mother and Father. They all mounted and made straight for the road to Nevern. They picked their way down the hillside very gingerly, until the horses were on the tarmac of the B road.

Eri waved in farewell.

"I must return to the others. You are quite safe now, I think. May you come safely to journey's end."

He waved again and rode off in the opposite direction. Anir spurred his horse on and led Peter and Sarah and their very surprised parents to Dinas, via Newport. By the coast the sun was shining on the beaches as if it had never been away.

Tourists thronged the town of Newport and no one had noticed the great battle on the Prescelly Mountains.

"Wasn't it awful weather yesterday?" was all that was remarkable to them, it seemed! "What a great storm!" they said.

Anir's party remained silent. Mother and Father were truly astonished. They had been packing up archaeological items into the boxes they had brought with them to the Summer School. Their enforced removal and sudden transformation to the wet mountaintops of Pembroke had caused them to think a great deal. As they rode into Dinas, all sorts of questions were forming in Mother's head.

All Sarah wanted to know was: Aunt Myf; where was she? Was she still safe and sound in the halls of Arx Emain? It was no good asking Anir now but when he left them at the top of the drive that led to Aunt Myf's cottage, she whispered her anxious query to him.

He tried to reassure her by saying that he was sure all was well, and Sarah gave him a big hug. Anir withdrew his arm sharply.

"Oh I'm so sorry, you're hurt."

" It's nothing," said Anir, "but don't squeeze me so hard!"

Then he shook Peter very warmly by the hand.

"Don't you need some attention to your arm, Mr. Anir?" said Mother.

This was the first time that she had spoken since being deposited on top of the mountain.

"No, thank you. I shall be quite all right very soon. It will not take me long to get back. Indeed, I really must be going. Farewell to you all for the present."

Anir bowed from his horse and clattered down the road to Arx Emain as fast as he could go.

"Well!" said Father, looking at Peter with 'eyeball to eyeball contact', "I think you have some explaining to do!"

"And the first thing," thought Sarah, "is to explain what has happened to Aunt Myf!"

They came all too soon to Aunt Myf's cottage. The door had been replaced but still bore the signs of the attack by Orddu's creatures. The horses they left outside to graze, having tied the reins to their saddles.

Sarah found a spare key under a shell in the garden. She opened the door.

"What on earth has been going on?" said Mother, "And where's my sister?"

"Um, Er..." said Peter, dumb with embarrassment.

But fortunately for him this question was answered almost immediately with a ring of the telephone. Father took the call, then said to Mother:

"Your sister appears to be in the Willow Tree hospital at Haverfordwest."

"WHAT!" yelled Mother.

Peter and Sarah could not imagine what had gone on.

"It seems there was a burglary a week or two ago. Well, while these two were off gallivanting around doing goodness knows what! The thieves must have returned and 'bopped' Aunt Myf over the head. Apparently, they found her swimming in the local reservoir, suffering loss of memory."

"Amnesia?" said Peter.

"Bless you," said Mother, who thought he had sneezed.

"That was an Inspector Davies. Sergeant Emmanuel was meant to be keeping an eye on Aunt Myf. He obviously failed dismally and Inspector Davies is deeply apologetic. Aunt Myf finally came round this afternoon at about four p.m."

"Just when the Samildanach left through the portal," thought Peter, "but how did she get out of Arx Emain? At least they did the trick, though, and she got rescued."

"I'll have to go at once!" said Mother, "Have you got your wallet?"

"Fortunately, I have!" said Father, "I'll call a taxi at once."

Mother made tea while they waited for the taxi to arrive. When it came, all she said was

"You can explain everything to your Father. I can hear it all later when I've sorted out Aunt Myf."

And then she was gone, having first relieved Father of all the cash in his wallet because, with the suddenness of their forced journey, her handbag had got left behind.

It took Peter and Sarah the rest of the evening to even begin to explain to Father what had gone on. He was very good about it. He was used to ancient relics and mythology and so some of it was not entirely strange to him. He also saw at once that they were telling the truth.

When Peter got as far as the day before the battle, it was eleven o'clock and he sent them to bed. Then Mother phoned from the hospital, where she was going to stay the night. Apparently Inspector Davies had felt so bad about it all, that he had turned up at visiting time with flowers for Aunt Myf and they seemed to get on very well! Mother said:

"She can't remember anything, though, except waking up in the hospital."

When Father told Peter and Sarah this the next morning, he could see that they were very pleased.

"I think it has all worked out for the best," he said, "I shall tell Mother only what she absolutely needs to know, at first. If Aunt Myf really has amnesia, I think we'll leave her part out of it. It would only upset your Mother more than she is already. However, she will have to KNOW ALL eventually. Tell the truth and shame the Devil, that's what I say."

Mother came back the next day.

"I think that Inspector Davies has taken a shine to our Myfanwy!" she said happily, "I just left him with her again. 'All part of our enquiries' he said, but he'd brought a box of chocolates with him."

"Oh good! I scent an engagement, definitely an engagement!" smiled Sarah.

Aunt Myf did not return the next day but when Mother visited her that evening, Sister said she could leave the following afternoon. They all spent the rest of that day making preparations for her homecoming.

The whole cottage was spring-cleaned. Father did the garden, Peter went into Cwm-yr-Eglwys for supplies, and Sarah filled the rooms with flowers. Father went with Mother in the taxi to fetch her. When they returned, no one mentioned Elves or Stones or anything like that.

After a large tea Aunt Myf went to her bedroom to rest.

"Thank you all so very much! Thank you, thank you!" she beamed over the banister, "You must all stay the rest of the week."

"Hurray!" shouted Peter and Sarah, "Can we?" -- their eyes pleaded with Mother and Father.

"Of course," said Mother.

And that was that. Father had already phoned to the University and explained their sudden removal with perfect truth as 'owing to a family emergency.' Real term at University did not begin for ages after school started, so there was plenty of time for a holiday.

Mother and Father bought themselves spare clothes and other things that had been left behind, like toothbrushes! Then they all had the most wonderful week. They bathed, watched seals, visited mediaeval castles, went shopping in Haverfordwest, saw 'Planet battles, Volume 1: The Ghostly Threat' at the local cinema.

Though it has to be said they found it rather tame after all they had been through. And they took the boat to Skomer Island to see the puffins. Inspector Davies, whose other name was Tomos came for dinner and they all decided that they liked him, especially Aunt Myf. He was still mystified over Aunt Myf's burglary.

"We'll catch them one day," he said.

All too soon it was time to go home and get ready for school again and Peter and Sarah had seen no sight or sound of any Elf or of Anir. Of course there was no going home by car, as it had not been brought.

"Very irritating!" moaned Father, when he discovered how much the train fare was going to be.

The morning of the twelfth dawned. Aunt Myf felt well enough to see them off at the station. The taxi took them all, but Inspector Davies came to take Aunt Myf home! They waved and waved their good-byes.

"Come again soon!" called Aunt Myf.

But none of the family realised just how soon that would be.

CHAPTER NINE

The Ninth Wave

That term at school, Peter and Sarah were unsettled. Everyone noticed it. Then just before Christmas, Mother came into their rooms to tell them that Aunt Myf was going to be married.

"To that nice Inspector?" asked Sarah.

"Yes. And then they will go to live in Newport."

"What will happen to the cottage?" said Peter.

"Well, your Father and I have a surprise for you."

By this time they were all sitting on Sarah's bed. She called Father in.

"You tell," he said.

"Father applied to work for the University of Wales at Aberystwyth, so we shall need somewhere to live, not too far from there as they have given him a Professorship."

"Great!" said Peter.

"Fantastic!" said Sarah.

The wedding was set for the week after Christmas. They all went to Aunt Myf's for the celebration and to help with the wedding preparations. It was the best Christmas ever.

Then the day of the wedding approached, the Saturday after Christmas. It was cold, but not bitterly cold. Father was to give Aunt Myf away, Peter and Sarah were page and bridesmaid and Mother was, naturally, maid of honour.

As Sarah looked in her jewel case, for something to match the deep blue of the velvet bridesmaid's dress, she fumbled about and discovered:

"The ring!" she gasped, "The ring of concealment."

She ran to find Peter. They had not spoken much of the events of the preceding summer, as there had been far too much to think about in the present.

"Anir's ring!" she said, "What shall I do with it."

"Let's wait and see," said Peter, straightening his tie.

"You look funny," Sarah giggled.

Peter sighed.

"So do you. No, I don't mean that. You look fine."

Sarah replaced the ring among her jewelry and they left for the church.

Later, as the official photographer was posing them all: Aunt Myf resplendent in oyster satin and Tomos in his topper and tails, Peter and Sarah found themselves momentarily standing by an old yew.

"I'm freezing, Peter."

"So am I. Let's go back in the church."

They were just about to do so, when someone cleared his throat behind them, someone standing behind the tree.

"Anir!" they gasped.

"Yes! And it's good to see you two again."

"We've got so much to ask," whispered Peter.

"Well, I may one day have the time to tell you all the answers," said Anir "but not now. Come to the ruins of the Bishop's Palace at St. David's at twilight on May the first, next year."

"Is it your wedding?" asked Sarah.

"It is!" replied Anir, grinning from ear to ear, "But you had better get back to this one. It wouldn't do for you to be seen talking to a tramp, now would it? Go on!"

Anir winked at them.

"Remember! May first, twilight."

And he disappeared silently. Aunt Myf and her new husband were getting into their limousine and Mother and Father were waving at Peter and Sarah to 'come on'.

The wedding feast passed merrily. The weeks passed and the months. Peter and Sarah went to a new school, locally. Peter began a coin collection. No more stones for him!

Father's new job went very well and he said that his new book was to be about Ancient Greece and that they would all be going there in the summer.

"We've learnt our lesson," he said.

And Mother joined in:

"Yes, as far as possible in the future, all our holidays will be family holidays. We shall be keeping a strict eye on both of you from now on."

In April Aunt Myf began a bump that was to turn into Catrin. She did not go back to the study of Ancient Celtic history, but joined the horticultural society instead.

Mother spent her time, after she had done the cottage over, typing up Fathers books on the computer.

"Got to keep up with the new technology, haven't I?" she said.

Then came the end of April and Peter and Sarah took Father on one side and told him about Anir and the invitation.

"Please! Oh please let us go!" they said, "Just this once!"

Father agreed, if it was 'just this once'. But he had his suspicions. At any rate, 6 p.m. on May Ist found the four of them, for Mother had been persuaded to come also, parking the car just outside the Cathedral at St. David's.

They went to the ruins and under the glimmer of the first stars, saw a grand procession of the most beautiful people.

"Ellyllon, Elves, The Family of Beauty," muttered Father, as he held Mother tightly by the hand.

The ceremony had obviously taken place at Arx Emain. This was the procession to the honeymoon. The family followed. Aneryn was radiant in a white and silver gauze gown, studded with jewels. Anir wore cloth of gold and golden armour nearly as bright as that of Gwyn-ap-Nudd and his brother, Ederyn, who was now recovered from his wounds.

As they passed Sarah and Peter, Anir paused momentarily.

"We meet again, my friends! Our thanks to you on this most joyous occasion," he said.

"Why do you thank us?" Peter asked, in great surprise.

"Because," replied Aneryn, "if you had not found the Stone of Gardar, Arddu might not have been defeated and it would not have been safe for us to marry."

"And I would not have passed the test!" said Anir, "I had to prove myself worthy of Aneryn before Gwyn and all his people."

Here Gwyn, who was standing to one side of the happy couple, bowed low and smiled.

"So you see," continued Aneryn, "all has come right as would not have done, had you not found the Stone. But come, dearest Anir, we are delaying the celebrations. Our ship awaits. Farewell friends!"

"Farewell friends!" Anir called, "Until we meet again!"

Then he and Aneryn waved and smiled and then passed on and down to the beach. There they went aboard a ship shaped like a silver swan.

Gwyn and the rest of the wedding party went aboard also. But as the ship made ready to sail, Aneryn leaned over the bow and threw her bouquet to – Sarah!. The rest of the Elves waved and cheered and then departed homewards, singing. Their song was one of homage to Anir and Aneryn.

> The trees were bare, the year was old,
> When fate found Anir wandering.
> His cloak was grey, his brooch was gold,
> The snow lay thick and glistening.

> As he walked on, he heard a sound,
> The trees too, they were listening,
> He crossed a stream and on a mound
> Anir saw moonlight glimmering.

> Upon the mound a maiden lay,
> All Elvish beauty mirroring.
> The many stars above her gaze
> Soft light in her hair shimmering.

> A cold wind blew, Aneryn woke.
> For it was she who was sleeping.

Anir came close and softly spoke,
    The love within him leaping.

They left the mound and forest glade.
    The frosty woods were shivering.
And doom fell on Aneryn then,
    As with Anir she went journeying.

Hard and long was the way they trod,
    'Til at last one fate remaining
Bore them across ever widening seas,
    In a ship, all joys containing.

The Elves passed back through the Bishop's Palace ruins.
"Farewell Anir, Farewell Aneryn! Joy to you!" they called.
"Farewell, Anir and Aneryn," whispered Peter and Sarah.

Then they too turned their faces homewards, Mother and Father leading the way back to the car park.

As they sat in the back of the car, Sarah said, quietly,

"He has joined the Elves for ever now. I don't think we will see him again."

A tear dropped into Aneryn's bouquet of ferns and lilies of the valley.

"Let's wait and see," said Peter, and squeezed his sister's hand "Remember, you still have the Ring of Concealment."

"So I do," whispered Sarah, and her face brightened.

The two of them then remained silent for the rest of the journey, pondering much on all that they had seen.

The End